Desert Skies

By

Csilla Toldy

PublishAmerica
Baltimore

ISBN: 1-4241-1658-9
PUBLISHED BY PUBLISHAMERICA, LLLP
www.publishamerica.com
Baltimore

Printed in the United States of America

For Jeremy

'The Soul never thinks
without a mental image.'
—Aristotle

Intro

I was sixteen when I first met Jeremy. He struck me as a crazy, ruthless bonvivant, the romantic hero of an operetta, but also as a very fragile young man who had a much stronger expressed need for love than anybody I knew. We became like siblings. I was the younger one; nevertheless it felt that I was his big sister, looking after my reckless little brother's interests. I had to protect him from girls. He had many and changed them frequently like other people change their shirts. His method was simple; with every breath and every move he was telling them 'I don't want you,' which made them crazy, magnetized. They hung on him like bees on honey, but when they realized that he had been truthful to them, they became embittered.

I forgave him, instead of them. To return my act of love he told me his story, as an explanation for his restlessness. He talked to me about CC and her death.

Jeremy died on my seventeenth birthday and I did not go to his funeral. I could not accept his death for ten years. When I did, I went to see his sister who, quite magically, was already expecting me with love letters and photographs to help to write his story. I changed names, settings, backgrounds,

5

affirming my belief that this story could be happening anywhere, anytime.

The real protagonists of this novel are now in the desert. Its fictional heroes are still alive, somewhere in the universe.

Gerry

A young man was sitting on his motorbike at the railway crossing near Lurgan. It was nearly the end of twilight, the seven o'clock Translink express from Belfast to Dublin was due to run past there any minute. His narrow eyes were searching the distance where the rails disappeared, piercing into the mist that softened the last shimmers of the day. His grayish white skin under the dark hair completed the black and white landscape, like a link in a chain.

It seemed as if he was impatiently drumming with his fingers on the steering. In fact, he was playing an imaginary clarinet in an orchestra, in harmony with the Lurgan River, the mellow whispering trees, the discreetly gossiping birds and the humming motorbike.

Gerry could hear the symphony in his head, until he became aware of the approaching train, at last. First it was just a low murmur in the back of his mind, not much different from the rushing blood in his veins. As it got closer and more perceptible, the sound slowly subdued all the other noises, until there was nothing else, but violent power.

He saw the lights of the engine growing into his face, heard the high-pitched whistle and the squealing breaks. He was thrilled to the bones.

Why? Perhaps, his friends were right when they called him an adrenaline-junky, but there was more to it. He needed to go to the edge, swing like an acrobat above the abysmal darkness, and glimpse at the face of whoever was beyond.

'I know you're a friend.'

'Yes, we speak the same language.'

'Is that enough?'

'It's more than enough.'

'Who are you then, tell me.'

'I am your inheritance from the ancestors, the forecast shadow on the way ahead. I'm always with you.'

'Then why do I need to test you again and again?'

'Because you're frightened.'

'No, I'm not, just watch me.'

Gerry had this strange passion of waiting for the express train at the railway crossing, sitting on his motorbike. He wanted to reach his own limits, to find out how close could he let the train come before he ran for his life. The engine was ready to jump off any moment; he was not risking too much, just enough to get high. He did this once a month, sometimes once every week, depending on his mental state, till he realized that the train drivers must have been warned, for they started to slow down when they were approaching the crossing. To add to his worries one night he just narrowly escaped being caught by a police patrol that was hiding behind a derelict farmhouse. He enjoyed the chase, but it made him think twice nevertheless, before he came to meet his imaginary friend again. He did not want to cause his ma too much bother.

He could not totally give it up; however, the need to test his own courage was deeply imbedded into his genetic blueprint. He came from a lineage of officers and his father had been an SAS man. The world saw Gerry as a half-orphan, but he knew more than the world. His father could never be dead as long as he lived, his memory continued living in him. He owed this incredible and inconceivable man not only his life, his name, his fantasies, but also his responsibilities as a big brother of Liam and the protector of their ma. Deep down in his soul, he was always grateful to Barry Tanner, even when he was angry with him for having abandoned them when he died.

He was an officer of the Special Air Service, a member of the notorious secret army, made of the toughest men in Britain. They were sent to Northern Ireland to fight terrorism. 'Who Dares Wins,' 'Strike and Destroy,' 'Descend to Defend' were their mottos. Gerry could picture his cloth cap badge, the winged dagger, derived from Excalibur, designed in Cairo. In his early boyhood Gerry wanted to get it tattooed into his arm, and he would have got it done, no doubt, if tragic circumstances had not made him think twice. His idolized father knew a lot about termination and survival, balancing always on the thin line between life and death.

Gerry's story began in the Troubles of the mid-nineteen eighties, the day Barry met Marie, and they fell in love. Their relationship could have become a sweet romance, written in heaven, if the curious fly had not famously committed suicide and jumped into the ointment: A British soldier and an Irish Catholic! In other parts of the world we could easily say 'and so what?' and we would be right, if they had not chosen the wrong place at the wrong time. Their innocent love stirred up monstrous hatred. Marie got pregnant; Barry married her, which meant that nobody from her family talked to her anymore.

Gerry was born in Belfast in a military hospital and immediately after his birth Barry took his young family to England. Marie's family would only forgive her for wedding a Brit Protestant soldier, when her husband died.

Barry had at least two professions. He was an electrician, and an aircraft mechanic, Gerry knew so much for sure.

Thanks to Barry, they lived in Egypt for a short period, when Gerry was about three. His mother could never tell him, why precisely, did they spend those years in the capital of Arabia.

'Your daddy got a job there, and I was the happiest woman in the world. We lived near the embassy and we made trips to exotic places on a motorbike with a sidecar.'

'I remember that.'

'You can't. You were only three.'

'I do remember. He was not a soldier there.'

'That's right. He worked at the embassy as an electrician.'

For Gerry the two years spent in Cairo became just another thread in the tapestry of a magic carpet; his imagination that could take him away.

While they were in Cairo the parents conceived Gerry's brother, Liam, and their father died shortly after their return to England, when Liam was about one.

Gerry had to learn very early that time was a relative commodity and eternity just a second. It was the same unit of time he needed to get off the rails before an express train hit him, a flash.

In the coming years, Barry Tanner lived on in Gerry's fantasies. Gerry pictured his father as a spy in Cairo, being a double agent, working for the Pentagon and the KGB at the same time, handling information in a way and with such speed that only he could grasp. He was party to secret missions, searching for ancient treasures and the weapons of the aliens that were hidden in the catacombs of the pyramids, adventurer and crusader, a sort of Indiana Jones and King Arthur in one body. His Holy Grail was the balance between the opposing forces, to help achieve peace in the world. He had become so disillusioned with Britain's role in Northern Ireland that he devoted himself to world peace in Egypt—it sounded pretty far-fetched, but it all made perfect sense to Gerry, at least. He told and retold this sheer assumption so many times to Liam, and himself and to all his buddies and enemies that it became his Bible. At the age of ten, three years after his father's death Gerry was so much enmeshed in his heroic spy father's stories, mostly set around Cairo and the desert that he could easily recite them for hours. They had a ring of truth, and they were as strongly present in his memory as the real impressions he had in the dirty streets of Cairo.

Bold and sensual Arabia happened to Gerry at the age when children start to gather memories. Life suddenly became much louder and it smelled different. It was much more intense than he had ever known before in grey and damp England. The streets were market places where everybody was selling and buying and beggar-musicians played music, street entertainers blew fire and people were shouting at each other whilst listening to the radio. His memory was alive with huge ice-white walls reaching up into the velvety blue sky. Buzzing streams of flies whirled up the heat heavy from the exhaust fumes of cars. His heart beat to the rhythm of the Nile that used to come up to the city people's feet and flooded the streets.

He would never forget the feeling he had when he was first listening to the undulating melody of Arabian music, even though with the passage of time the images became more and more like a restoration of an old film about Arabia. He was a boy of four, sitting in the Cairo dust, in the middle of dried-up excrements in between goats' hooves, rotten vegetables and the usual waste of packaged civilization, his image distorted by the exhaust fumes and swirling heat. Above him, plump market women were mounting against the sky, wearing their traditional long black chuddar, their faces hidden, only showing their burning eyes, wildly gesticulating, shouting at each other in Arabian, probably bargaining. To his amazement, the commotion became part of the music and it slowly subdued every other noise. He was overfilled with joy and excitement, amused and amazed. Something new was going on inside his thin cotton trousers. He looked down to investigate the course of events, and discovered the immense power of music, the heat rising in between his pencil-shape legs, dancing like a serpent.

This early sexual experience, so strongly intertwined with the music, became one of the most important impressions of his life as a youth. It planted the seed that would develop into a love of music, which became an all-pervading passion so that he eventually had to decide to become a musician.

Strangely, that moment in the sand also imprinted his attitude to women. Like those Arabian ladies in their dark gowns, girls irresistibly attracted his interest, but only as long as their secret was hidden and he was compelled to play to seduce. When the music was over and they allowed him to glimpse behind their veils, he suddenly felt deflated, ready to move on.

Home Sweet Home

Life abruptly changed for the Tanners after Barry's death. Marie was still very young; she had been only eighteen when she met Barry. She was beautiful with her raven black hair and blue eyes, her grief made her inner beauty shine through even stronger. She could never wear her attractive looks with ease, she felt terribly vulnerable in the company of strangers. Barry had provided for her, not only the basics of life, but he was the source of her friends and family alike. Suddenly, without the support of her husband she felt alien as an Irish woman in England. As she had never finished her studies, she could only do manual jobs and the prospect of having to raise her two boys all alone cast an enormous shadow over her.

One day she decided to go home from England. She knew in her guts that her roots would never deny her and she was right. Her clan accepted her and her children without resentment as if the distance that Marie's seven-year exile created had never existed. The people who stayed did not change; they were still the same tribal community she left behind. Gerry and Liam felt alien in their new world, while Marie was if not comfortable, but at home in her past.

Nevertheless, she found it just as hard to cope with their new, much drearier life in West-Belfast, where everybody seemed to be hiding behind high walls, bars and barricades. They were surrounded by metal and concrete, even the tap water was brownish with its iron content. Gerry acquired a metallic taste in his mind: of corrugated iron gates, streets that could be closed down easily, walls, higher than two men, so that nobody could climb up, or cast explosives to the other side. Barbed wires topped the walls and fences; they often caught plastic bags that seemed to fly around, playing with the wind like butterflies in happier places. The partition walls were painted with elaborate graffiti, high quality popular art, depicting heroes of the republican movement, martyrs of the hunger strikes, masked men with rifles and machine guns. Marie's sons knew nothing about surveillance, yet they felt being watched all the time. The estate itself was a thousand eyed monster, it peeped at them from everywhere, from the pictures on the walls, from behind curtains in the windows, from the keyholes in the doors, from the cracks in the fences, and from the curves in the Celtic cross in the cemetery. People seemed to know everything about them, while they knew nobody. Worse, everybody seemed related with everybody else; they were a big family, while the Tanners were the outsiders, the friends of the enemy. The army patrolled the streets in riot vans, and they made their terrifying presence unmistakable in deafeningly noisy helicopters.

In this Catholic ghetto of the city people had the capacity to remember, even longer than elephants. Marie still had the stigma of the British soldier's whore. The prisoner wives and the widows of the volunteers of the Irish Republican Army spat on their front door when they walked by.

They could never be really sure who did or did not belong to this no-face army, for whenever they publicly appeared they wore masks. In West-Belfast they were powerful and omnipresent. Fear was a good soil for the seeds of terror, and hatred grew out of it. Keeping these two evils alive in the hearts of people was means enough to keep them under control. Of course, the oppressed did not realize that they were the victims of their own making. Instead they maintained the comforting belief that their big brothers who unlike them, were brave enough to use the guns, protected them. Later Gerry realized that this was true for both sides. The Protestants expected to be protected by the British soldiers, but they had the law on their side, which made them feel superior, while being thoroughly and deeply scared.

In those early days in West-Belfast, Gerry did not think much about this. He was simply crippled by the harshness of the experience. Five years old Liam became so clingy that he always wanted to stay indoors, and he could not be left alone in any of the rooms inside the house. He followed the adults like a lapdog.

One day, when the situation became untenable for everybody, the family council sat down around the kitchen table to discuss the Tanners' future.

'I cannot bear how the neighbors treat us anymore,' Old Mrs. Murphy said wearily.

'It's more serious than that, Maggie. Your daughter's life is in danger,' Mr. Murphy interrupted her with a growl.

'What? Did you hear anything?' asked his wife, trembling.

'It's not that bad yet, but you remember old Julie O'Hare. When they found out that her husband had been a prod she just disappeared without a trace.'

'Yes, what a waste. She had six children for God's sake.'

'That's right. Marie, you and the boys must leave here, before it's too late.' Mr. Murphy turned to Marie, who was rigidly listening as if she was a witness in a court case.

'We just arrived. Where could we go? To the south?'

'Joe, we must ask your sister. She is such a good soul she might be even happy to have somebody there now that she is so ill,' said Mrs. Murphy, meaning her husband's sister, Maeve.

To the children's despairing relief, they had to move again, because of the sins of their mother and father, because of their love for one another. Gerry felt the loathe and discrimination on his own skin, and slowly he began to realize how proud he should be of his mother, what a real rebel she had been when she had followed her heart against all that fierce opposition in her environment. In later years, when he was old enough to ponder about the world in metaphysical terms and his own defining role in it, Gerry questioned Marie about her love and rebellion.

'Ma, tell me, how could you fall in love with the enemy?'

'First, he did not wear a uniform, for he was working undercover, but even so I think I would have fallen in love with him, anyway. Your dad had something about him that I couldn't resist. What I did later was sheer consequence. It wasn't such a big deal, I was in love and love never asks questions, Gerry.'

The simplicity of this statement ran like a shiver down on Gerry's spine. It made him wonder what the power of love would make him do one day.

They moved to the outskirts of Lurgan, exactly twenty miles from Belfast to Auntie Meave. She lived in an old farmhouse with a huge stable at its back.

Auntie Maeve never had children, and Gerry could understand why her husband had died so early, death being the most honorable way out of a miserable marriage. She might have been pretty when she was a young girl, but her character spoilt her looks. She was small and very thin, always rushing around like a Hurley stick. Her tongue moved as well all the time, even faster than her feet and the words shot out of her mouth like bullets.

She had cancer in its later stages. When Gerry got to know her better, with his cruel, childish honesty he thought that God gave her a fair reward, by giving her this terrible disease.

Although she was ill and they were obviously sent there to look after her, she did her utmost to show the Tanners her superiority. It was clear from the first moment of their arrival that they were a wicked family much in the need of improvement. She let everybody know, including her neighbors, doctors, caregivers, salespeople, church community and friends if she had any that she only took on the case of the Tanners for charity. Gerry guessed what her real intentions were. She was hoping to buy a ticket to Heaven in the last minute before her departure. Not as if she needed one, just to be on the safe side.

She started with the children. She cloaked her mission too well, so that Marie did not notice any of her plans. Perhaps, she was glad to have some spare time to herself on Sunday mornings.

'Children need guidance, all decent people know that.'

'Gerry, Liam, I need to take you to Sunday mass. There you can meet other good children, and you will be given some sweeties. How about that? Go now and put on some nice clean clothes.'

In the church she then approached her real life hero; father McKenzie, very worried about the fact that neither of the boys was christened.

'No problem, Sister Maeve, that's easily sorted. Bring them to learn the catechisms and I will christen them in due course.'

Poor young Liam got most of her loving care. He was only four and did not have the escape route to school, neither could he defend himself with homework nor flute lessons as Gerry could. One day Auntie Maeve secretly took Liam to Father McKenzie and got him christened.

Gerry escaped and he informed his mother about Auntie Maeve's meddling. This was the only time Gerry saw his mother bursting with fury, and fighting for her children like a lioness. She screamed at Auntie Maeve:

'It was my husband's wish to bring them up outside religion, and I will never forget that. He is with God, you remember?'

Aunty Maeve had nothing to add to this, she would never take God's name in vain, even if she thought that Barry had been thrown to Hell: Death had the highest authority in Ireland.

Gerry's father's wish was the reason why his ma sent him to a mixed secondary school in Belfast when he was twelve. It meant two hours of travel every day, but it was worth the while, for the school was good at music and the arts. He learned to play other wind instruments and music changed his life. Most probably, the confrontation with Auntie Maeve opened his mother's eyes and made her wish stronger to stay out of any sectarian debates. Gerry should have been grateful to Auntie Maeve, after all, but he did not have the wisdom of an old soul there and then yet. He could only see and ironically note that Auntie Maeve's meddle had its good sides, for he and his brother never had to go to church again.

Their home was a longish shaped stone house with two small bedrooms, a lounge and a kitchen. Auntie Maeve had nobody to spend money on. This is how Gerry explained the luxury of a bathroom installed some twenty years before they moved there and the disgusting fact that it was pink all over.

There was a niche in the kitchen, a doorway to the back of the house. It opened to a neglected storage barn full of rubbish, rabbit cages and hay, remainders, probably from the previous century.

During their first years in Northern Ireland, for Liam and Gerry this useless barn became a paradise. They played spy games under the barren roofs in the semi-darkness, hiding between the clutter and under the hay, scouting and chasing each other till they got tired of it. The barn's dangerous jungle soon became their real home. It offered them a place where they could cautiously avoid the rigorously cleaned and disciplined front yard that had only one purpose: to show to the town that its owner, Auntie Maeve was going to heaven. They often hid from Auntie Maeve in the 'Desert,' as they called the barn at the back. This magical playground had the capacity of changing its shape and qualities at the wink of an eye. While it was a war field crammed with invisible lurking enemies, it could easily turn into a protective mellow haven of high grass and flowers blanketed by a blue sky of flapping butterflies within seconds.

Liam always thought highly of Gerry. He was in a sense the substitute for their father, whom Liam could not remember. He was a toddler when their father died. For Liam, it was an exotic fact that he was born in Cairo, in the shadow of the pyramids and near the Arabian deserts, though he had no recollection of it whatsoever. All the knowledge he got about the time around his birth was brought to him by his brother and this was much nicer than all the later birthday celebrations he had.

His birthday meant a problem, for it fell on the eighth of July, just a few days before the national holiday of Northern Ireland. The twelfth of July was there to celebrate the Battle of the Boyne that William of Orange won sealing the fate of Ireland for centuries. Unfortunately, in each year in July people carried on fighting the same battle that their ancestors fought some two hundred years before. Thus his birthdays went under in fear and anger that crept into their house through the cracks in the walls. They could not go to the movies and it was advisable to stay at home all the time. Gerry brought some light into those days with the stories about Liam's birth, about their dad and mum in Egypt. They used to escape and play spy-games in the stall. Gerry often described the desert skylines to him with the many shades of yellow orange red and white and jokingly he said that Liam had brought with him the colors of the desert by having red hair. This gave Liam a hidden strength that he could draw on when he was teased for his flame-red hair at school.

The women in the house, Auntie Maeve and Marie, both reacted to the desert in different ways, but with similar denial. One day, to the boys' amusement they discovered that the good old lady dreaded to follow them into the barn. She stopped at the door in the kitchen that connected the barn to the house. She wavered pointlessly, her mind like a feather in the wind, then turned back and sat down in her living room to rest.

For their mother the barn presented a domestic problem.

'Gerry, Liam, I hate that useless door there. Come and help me.'

'Yes, Mum,' they said like young soldiers to the admiral.

'We will move the red sofa from the lounge and push it before it. Gerry, go and get that old tapestry from my cupboard, would you? We will hang it in front of that ugly door.'

The old tapestry was actually a patchwork rug that she had sown in the local women's group in the previous year, picturing a lame peace dove over the roofs of Lurgan.

Auntie Maeve died a year after they moved into her house. They had a wake for her and Gerry and Liam remembered to say only good things about her to strangers and family members coming from all over the country. Ma warned them to wipe out all the bad memories from their hearts:

'From now on you will only remember the good things about your auntie, understand?'

'Yes, and what were they?'

'Gerry! She left us a home, for God's sake.'

'Sorry, sir. You're right as always.'

'OK. We'll only remember the laughs,' intervened Liam, grinning at Gerry. So they did and they were utterly grateful to have a roof over their heads, which became a home by then, a home with a secret paradise.

After Auntie Maeve's funeral, Marie moved into her bedroom and Gerry continued to share the other one on the upper level with Liam. Ma's bedroom was just as crowded as the lounge. Little light could sneak in through the small window and it was immediately absorbed by the two big cupboards, and the large bed, an armchair, the toilet table and the old and faded carpets and pictures that covered the floor and the walls. The old furniture originally belonged to Auntie Maeve and it still smelled of her, after many years. Whenever their mother was given hope for a pay-raise she promised them and herself that she would buy new beds, but these promises, and many others that required money remained unfulfilled.

Life was much lonelier without Aunt Maeve, but also much more peaceful. Marie frequently sent her children to visit the grannies in West-Belfast. She regarded this as paying off her duties, but she never accompanied them. She could never forgive her family for banishing her when she married Barry. Liam thought that it lay in her nature to burn the bridges behind herself, and later he would discover the same trace in Gerry, as if they were carrying and nurturing their real enemies deep inside.

Liam knew from Gerry that their mother did the same trick after their father's death, when she sent back all his belongings to his parents in England. She cut them off and they never came to visit, not even around Christmas. Liam was sorry for having no family connections with their grandparents in England, but Gerry defended Marie.

'We have to love our ma for what she is.'

'But she cuts off everyone. I would really like to meet Dad's parents. Imagine the officer granddad; he must have been extremely proud of Da getting into the SAS.'

'Yeah, but with Da gone we don't know whether they liked Ma. I suspect they didn't. It could well be that Ma felt like a stranger in the Brit family.'

Liam could see that himself: their father came from a long lineage of army officers and their mother was just a Catholic from West-Belfast. Out of shyness or rather pride, no matter why, she chose to be reserved with them instead of building a relationship.

Their maternal grandparents in Belfast treated them as if they had never had a father. While other orphans in the streets of West-Belfast—and there were many—were allowed to mention or idolize their fathers, even if they were prisoners, Gerry and Liam had to shut up about their father. Whenever they arrived for a weekend, their grandmother reiterated the warning:

'If anyone asks you, your name's Murphy. Gerald Murphy and Liam Murphy, remember?'

This rule became their motto, and getting off the train in Belfast they ritually gave the five to each other shouting 'hello Murphy.' This protection proved to be essential, even though for Gerry it seemed as cowardice. His rebellious blood wanted to find out otherwise and consequently, they had an incident at the time when Liam was about ten and Gerry was fourteen.

It was the end of the summer term, the end of June, and they were staying for the weekend with the grannies. On Saturday afternoon they went to see a movie in the middle of the city. There were no omnibuses to West-Belfast. They had to take a taxi bus, which was a black cab shared by passengers who had the same destination. The first time they had traveled in such a cab, Liam really loved it, for they had none the like in Lurgan, but later he grew to dislike it. The spooky silence of the people crushed together inside really scared him. He did not tell this his brother. He did not want to disappoint Gerry; he wanted to be known as the brave fighter of the sand dunes, after all.

Liam felt similarly uncomfortable on their way home that afternoon, but as always, the taxi driver switched on the radio and eagerly listened to the radio presenter's forced jokes on Radio Ulster, like all the other passengers.

They got off at their corner and walked into their street. *Nearly safe at home,* he thought, when somebody shouted their real name:

'Tanner!

The blood stopped in Liam and he stood paralyzed, while Gerry turned around, trying to locate the person who called, but saw nobody. Liam suddenly felt very spooky again and started to run towards his grannies' house that was only a few yards away. When he looked back from half the way, he saw Gerry doing the contrary.

He was nearing an iron gate, the entrance to an empty site. They used to play soccer there sometimes, but only the two of them. The voice must have come from the field, he was right, but why did he need to investigate it, Liam did not comprehend. He stopped in the safety of the grannie's front yard and called after his brother:

'Gerry, come home!'

Gerry turned his head towards him and waved, then disappeared behind the corrugated iron that covered the gate. Liam became very worried and ran into the house. Granddad was sleeping in front of the telly that had a golf play on. It took him a few minutes to wake him. Then he helped up the old man and led him into the street, trying to ignore his consistent shaking.

When they arrived to the field behind the iron gate they found Gerry lying on the ground. The corner of his mouth was bleeding, and he was holding on to his stomach, trying to stand up. Grandda scooped him under the shoulders and helped him to stagger home, while Liam was watching their back anxiously.

Strangely enough, in the safety of the house they did not talk about what had just happened to Gerry, the oldies seemed to take the incident as a matter of fact. Grandpa helped Gerry to wash his mouth, and escorted him to the sofa in front of the television. Grandma brought some lovely cookies she had prepared and they all buried the incident of Gerry's beating with the painless pleasure of cap cakes.

The Inheritance

Marie Tanner had difficulty to support herself and her children after her husband died. Unbeknown to her sons she was saving up the entire widow pension for their studies; she got herself a job in a textile factory in Belfast, and became a commuter. This was a big change considering that she had never worked before. While her husband was alive she had all the time to be a good mother, wife and homemaker. As new-born factory lass, she felt that she was failing in most of her roles, she felt guilty and stressed out, and she allowed her extreme worries around the boys' well-being to consume her nerves. Her insecurities annoyed Gerry greatly; therefore he tried to escape from the clutches of her love, and from her suffocating anxieties.

The push and pull force she experienced from her older son confused her even more. She often felt at the end of her tethers, but her friends from the women's group advised her to trust the innate bond every mother had with their firstborn that could never be taken away. No matter how much she prayed and trusted, she could see that their relationship was faltering, even though they loved each other. She did not seem to notice that Gerry was growing into a young man, prepared to be at her side to support her. To the contrary, and to his deepest disappointment she sought support from another man, finding refuge in a relationship that she hoped would help her to bear her burdening life as a single mother.

She met Seamus McMullan on the train, when he still had a job in Belfast. They used to travel together, and got to know each other better, as she told Gerry, trying to make it all look innocent.

The first time Gerry saw Seamus; his mother's would-be lover had thin, reddish brown long hair, heavy with grease, hanging scarcely over his collar. It was raining outside; therefore Gerry gave him the benefit of the doubt for being wet. His eyes were brown-green with deep black rings underneath; he had a big soft nose, fat lips. He had a strong Derry accent, he curled up the ends of his sentences in that lulling manner as if he was begging your agreement, but ordering you with the harshness of his words at the same time. A cigarette was hanging in the left corner of his mouth; this could have slowed his loose tongue down, as Gerry hoped, but no way. He was wearing an old suit over his beer belly and heavy, muddy boots on his feet. He had big frosty, redden, but weak looking hands that he only took out of his pockets to occasionally drop the ash of his cigarette. When they shook hands, Gerry thought he was pressing the life out of a jellyfish and his stomach turned inside out. He was clearly a softy, and did not invoke Gerry's respect at all. It did not matter how his mother and Seamus called their relationship, he knew that Seamus was his mother's boyfriend, and he had no idea how to respond to him. His mother kept stipulating that Seamus was 'just a good friend,' but even this softening made him furious, for he suspected that Seamus forced himself upon her with his slow, persuasive lulling.

In a way Gerry felt that Seamus usurped him. By the time he imposed himself upon the Tanners, Gerry had already established his realm with its special order. He was the king of the castle. Seamus brought chaos with him and Gerry often lost control, and very soon into the relationship he started to feel like a stranger in his own home.

Liam surrendered to Seamus quickly, without resistance. Firstly, Gerry felt resentment towards his brother, who was at his side in the desert, fighting the enemy against all odds, but simply forgot to be there for him in real life, when a much greater enemy entered their lives. After having lamely observed his behavior for a while, one night, after Seamus left, Gerry approached Liam to get to the bottom of his truancy.

'Liam, would you please tell me: what the hell do you like about Seamus?'

Liam put it simply as ever.

'I have never had a grown-up friend before, you know? To tell the truth I am really grateful to Mum for bringing him home.'

He did not say, but Gerry understood that he had never had a father either, so Gerry forgave him wisely, the boy was only seven, after all.

Later, when Seamus became a member of their family, and a serious partner for their mother, Liam's relationship with Gerry changed in some way. For Liam, there was finally a flesh and blood man who could play football and took him to the matches. Seamus was great to discuss football with; he sported the Celtic, just as Liam did. Seamus took Liam to the swimming pool and to places his mother would have never gone to, they fished on Lough Neagh and cycled in the forests. Seamus let Liam drive his car on some days and this utmost honor made him feel that he had found a friend.

Gerry never accepted the friendship Seamus offered. For him Seamus was the invader, the hostile force that aimed to take over their desert, but in fact neither Gerry nor Liam had talked about their imaginary play field to Seamus. It did not occur to Liam to invite him to the desert, for he was so different. He smelt of tobacco, sometimes of whiskey. He was real. Unlike his brother, Liam liked his realness. Gerry hated it. He condemned Seamus as a drinker and parasite who came to suck their mother's blood, which was in Liam's eyes a ridiculous accusation.

Gerry thought, all right, Liam might have needed a guardian, but he did not. For his part, it became a necessity to play petty games with his mother to get what he wanted, and looking back from a distance, they seemed like ugly blemishes, impairing the beauty of his soul.

He often used Seamus' inevitable presence in their life to blackmail his mother for this and that, but mostly for freedom. Better to say, if he did not want to be limited in any way, he called out Seamus' name loudly. He sensed his mother's guilt for having a new man after the death of their father, and he played at it. Gerry, being the outcome of Marie's first and probably only love, was the ghost of her happier times with Barry. Gerry echoed her feelings: no matter that his father had died, in Gerry's view Marie was still married to his dad, so she was in an adulterous relationship with Seamus. Gerry exploited her guilt shamelessly for his own benefit, but with time this became a kind of secret game between them that played a role in re-enforcing their bond, where Seamus did not have anything to say.

Gerry came across this powerful psychological weapon by serendipity. He was pretty young, about ten years old when it presented itself, just when Seamus first appeared in their life. Later on, it became automatic and meaningless like a Pavlovian effect: On hearing her lover's name from her son's mouth, which he expelled like a curse or a matter of disgust, Marie would startle and twitch and suddenly change the subject in her son's favor.

The fact that Gerry resembled his father often confused his mother, and she called out with surprise:

'Just like your father!' Gerry usually objected:

'No, it isn't true. The only thing I resemble him is my short-sightedness.'

'And you don't even wear your glasses. You'll go blind!'

'Ma, I'm not like him. I'm neither an electrician nor an aircraft mechanic. I don't work for the army and I haven't died yet!'

'Oh, Gerry, respect the dead.'

Reaching this position, he had to change the subject:

'When is Seamus coming?'

She would then twitch and reply as if speaking to a higher authority:

'At two o'clock.

'By that time I'll have gone, but give him my kindest regards.'

This used to be the moment when she started flattering:

'What shall I buy for you from my savings, dear?'

'Nothing, just allow me to repair that old motorbike.'

Here, somewhere, they could have reached the peak of tension in the conversation, where Marie had to decide whether her concerns or her inner need to bribe her son were stronger. She either agreed or carried on:

'Motorbikes're very dangerous.'

In any of these cases it was already decided that Gerry would win, thus he gave her a big kiss or thanked her nicely, or promised her to be careful, and so on.

This was, roughly, the story of how Gerry was allowed to drive his motorbike. It was an old, battered Triumph, the same make his father had in Cairo and Gerry found it in the desert. Finding it was one of those rare miracles in life. It seemed as if his father had left it for him there, but of course, this was not possible. Barry had never been in that house; he had not known anything about its existence.

The motorbike had been stored and getting rusty in the back barn of the house for ages, until Gerry repaired it with his friend, Lord. They oiled all its bits, painted the tank black. Gerry learnt to drive it and rode it from his sixteenth birthday on. It was slow, heavy and very loud, which he liked for the sake of the effect.

Naturally, it also used up all his pocket money, but he needed money to remain mobile. He took on many jobs, like window cleaning and music tuition, and he learnt the ropes of marketing himself. For the sake of the motorbike he became a living billboard on wheels, advertising his skills, boasting with his talents, bargaining. This went on for a while until he got the idea to start a rock band that was supposed to make him rich and famous one day. For many of his mates he was a scope, but there was no petrol in the world that the old sluggish bear would not soaked up, he had to feed him. They needed each other. The bike taught him the feeling of freedom, and God knows he was free when he was sitting on its back, patrolling the streets like a real stud.

Empowered by his inheritance, Gerry developed a sense for the unknown with incredible speed. Therefore, on the day he first met Saoirse, he could feel her approaching him from miles away.

He was waiting for his lunch in his mother's kitchen, contemplating some underground presentiments that were quivering in his bones and veins. Their alluring whisper augured the coming of some unbelievable event.

The glass in the front door was steamed up, blocking his view. Ma was excitedly stirring the stew, her ritual creation for Saturday lunch.

Their dog, 'Blacky,' was barking outside. He had the annoying habit of barking at anything that moved, shouting his suffocating fear into the world. They believed that he must have had a shock when he was a puppy, which was not unlikely, considering the madness that surrounded them in Lurgan.

Gerry jumped on his feet and peeped through the window, wiping it with the palm of his hand. He impatiently checked whether it was raining. It was the middle of February and he could not wait to ride his motorbike again. Blacky was barking at the neighbor's guests who had just arrived, extremely formally dressed, with a bottle of wine. The man in the dark suit pulled his face into a sad smile and rang the bell. Gerry could smell the sweet odor of the fat woman's patchouli, even through the window. John, their neighbor's eldest son, was killed the day before. He was only twenty-two and a police informant, or so it was, but now he was simply dead and he reserved the same respect as anybody else. Your day will come—this was the slogan of the IRA in Irish, and well, his day was there. People were arriving for the wake, mainly on foot. From their rigid slow motions and alert eye movements Gerry could sense the heavy presence of power. He searched around with his eyes and saw a blue car pulling up on the opposite side of the road. The driver switched off the engine and gazed intently on the couple entering the house. The other man took out a crinkled newspaper from the gloves department, getting ready to read—as if preparing for a long and boring stay. It was obvious that they were policemen.

When he was younger, Gerry had been friendly with John, but Marie had never let him go into his house. She instinctively tried to keep people in the neighborhood at distance, although she did not tell her children, why. She was probably frightened that 'they' would find them. No matter how naughty the boys were, they never doubted her instincts, for she always proved to be right.

Although a part of him was sad about John's tragic death, Gerry could see no reason to suppress his joyous excitement about the night to come. The weather was fine. He sat down at the long dining table, and started drumming on the plate, ready to leave within seconds.

Ma was standing at the oven next to the half-open kitchen door. The thin grey light coming through the slot enveloped her small figure. Her hair was black with a tint of blue like a raven's feather coat, and her eyes shiny blue. Gerry often thought that his mother's face looked really sexy for her age and the trauma she had to live through. In her eyes, hidden between the wrinkles, there was a pixy's naughtiness that was released when she laughed. Around the waist and hips she had a kind softness that Gerry loved to feel when he laid his arms around her.

'When do you think you will be back? I don't want to worry, Gerry.'

'Late. We are going to play tonight.'

'I don't see you during the week and you go out most of the weekend!'

'Don't' complain, Mum. You have Shimmy and Liam in my place.'

'They are not in your place!' screamed Marie at her son, but Gerry rushed to her and hugged her from behind.

He went to the disco on his Triumph that night, expecting the unexpected. The air was wet and fog began to spread when he finally finished his meal. He had to put on his father's old leather overall, almost the same age as himself. It had been brown originally. By that time, grey strips of mould spotted it here and there, especially at the elbows and the hollow of the knees. The ravages of time made the leather hard and stiff, so the overall sat like an elephant skin on him. People reacted in many different ways to his outfit. For many he looked like the ghost of a terrible Christmas. He could be sure that the police would stop him and ask for his papers every time he wore the overall, thinking he was a terrorist. Tramps usually stopped and spat as a sign of recognition, but it took Gerry a while to get the message that they only did it out of respect. Older women, including his mother crossed themselves with a dreadful face, and young girls stopped and watched him in amazement.

The High-Flyers

There was a Valentine Day's party at the biggest club in town, and the club owner, Billy Gates invited the High-Flyers to play once again. Billy was very cautious with the choice of his music and the boys knew how to value this recognition. In a practical sense putting the High-Flyers on his program was a brave step, for the High-Flyers were a mixed group that was going to play in a preliminary Protestant neighborhood. He had to make sure not to have any trouble in his disco. His choice conveyed the message to the people that he was non-sectarian and some people could have had problems with that, but for the boys this represented much more. Being accepted by Billy Gates meant that their music was good, worth risking a political statement.

This was the third time that they had a concert there and Billy even had High-Flyers on the posters. Although he gave them only half an hour to play, he must have become increasingly convinced that they would draw in customers. The boys, on the other hand, were looking forward to the possibility of pulling girls.

The club reminded Gerry of the inside of a horse stall, only the walls were painted black. The air was steaming with madmen, like tired horses after race. Most of the sweating heads started off towards the bar, while the DJ changed the obviously wild and exhausting house music into a milder rock. Gerry could glimpse a few pretty birds, but some stallions heavily guarded them. He went backstage straight, looking for his mates.

He found Lord and Leo in the changing room where they were checking their looks vainly in a dilapidated mirror. Lord's new jeans and his dark suede jacket could not hide his chubby legs and arms, although he even had tied a red scarf around his neck. His blue eyes lit up when he saw Gerry, and he playfully lifted his black Bogart hat. His blonde wiry hair became visible for a second, unwilling to be covered again by the ridiculous head-dress. No matter what he thought, Gerry kept his mouth shut, not wanting to make an acidic remark before the concert. He was cautiously keeping Lord's high spirits alive, in the interest of their shared success. Lord was the best guitar player he knew and he had to maintain a good relationship with him. Other than his music, he was a man of the masses, merely interested in the material values of life, like money and sex. Clearly, he was scared to go deeper below the surface, at least as long as his own feelings were concerned. He preferred to analyze other people, especially Gerry's inner world instead. Gerry took it as a challenge and tried to come before him whenever he could what often amused him, but on many occasions he just found it too stressful and wished that Lord would vanish.

Leo was short and bespectacled. He wore a turtle necked caftan in his beloved Indian style. This was his stage outfit and Gerry thought it suited his soft character rather well. He lived in Belfast, his parents were both doctors, and rich compared to Gerry's or Lord's. He was a good pianist, a keyboard player and a real expert in the history of music. He could be aloof and unapproachable, he could be so bloody highbrow, as Gerry thought, but he had a good heart. Gerry could always rely on Leo. Lord as the other pole was unpredictable; Gerry could never be sure when he would turn against him just in order to test his own strength. Gerry did not understand why Leo was inhibited, especially with girls. Perhaps, because he found it impossible to hide his sensitivity and intelligence, and unfortunately, these qualities were rather wasted with most of the girls according to Gerry's experience. The girls wanted sham and bravura. Gerry was able to mime these characteristics successfully, which gained him respect with his mates. Gerry knew that most of the girls saw him as a real stud and his friends had no reason to question his position, they rather looked up at him and appreciated his guidance in the matter of pulling girls.

Gerry was wearing his only pair of jeans. He did not have much else than this, except for a few old suits left behind by his father. Yet he was armed with his personality charm and embarrassingly good skills in causing confusion that used to serve him well.

When his friends saw him, it seemed he rescued the night for them; they both seemed suddenly resuscitated as if they had been given the kiss of life.

'Hello. I can see, you didn't dare out without me to the battlefield,' he said.

Leo blinked as he always did when he was excited:

'Let's concentrate on the music first, OK? We are on at nine thirty, I think it's too early, but Billy insists on it.'

'Nine thirty? Dead on, stop worrying. What about the birds?'

Lord switched on his usual provoking manner:

'All of them are waiting for you. Especially Vicky.'

Gerry looked at Leo expecting him to refresh his memory about Vicky, but Leo was miles away, sucking on his cigarette.

'Who is Vicky?' he asked him then. Leo woke up; seemingly bored he dropped the ash from his cigarette into the washbasin with a camp swing of his hand.

'You know, the gospel singer of Lurgan, you would know better, if you were a good sheep of God. And she's waiting for you as Lord assumed, but she might as well be waiting for Father Ted.'

The jackals indulged in their vicious laughter, obviously at Gerry's expense. After some hesitation he realized who they meant. Actually, Vicky lived just round the corner from Gerry's house. She had a strong, sexy voice that she used to the utmost bewilderment of the church going herd on Sunday Mass and most excitingly, she had the suitable set of breasts to go with that voice. Large, soft, intriguing, insulting! Everybody in the street had tried his luck with her, but she was more than choosy. Gerry guessed that she probably hated her excellent magnetic pillows; this must have been the reason why she chased away all the boys who dared to look at them. Though she seemed to be a hot number, Gerry had never approached her before. She reminded him too much of his mother's shape, but this time his mates challenged him and he had to defend his title.

'Oh, little brothers, I can tell from your baby giggle that you don't know anything about the depth of the female psyche. Let's bet that she really is waiting for me!'

The sound of money clicked on the businessman in Lord:

'I bet you ten quid that she tells you to go to hell, like she told the rest of us.'

They shook hands and Gerry let them enjoy their pre-empted success.

They went out and found Vicky, creating an obstacle with her large breasts in the corridor. She was standing with Billy, the club owner, under an old faded Guinness poster.

Her deep voice boomed over the background noise of the dance club. Gerry stopped, facing them and leaned against the cold wall. He began to gaze at Vicky, until she returned his look. They were discussing guys, inevitably. Vicky was confused by Gerry's stare, she continued talking, but turned to Gerry, which allowed Billy to give in to the urgent need to eye her breasts.

'The most disgusting thing about my generation is that the boys only think of sex. Their infantile heads are full of it.'

Leo and Lord were standing a little bit further off, but could still hear her deep resounding voice. They looked at each other knowingly and guffawed, almost managing to give Gerry away, he thought for a second. No sweat, he kept on glaring at her, then took out a piece of paper and wrote on it: 'Vicky, your voice is too good, let's try to play together.'

When Billy realized what she was talking about he seemed concerned that she might have put him in the same category as the boys of her age group. He forced himself to look straight into her eyes. Gerry knew he was desperately fighting to resist the magnetic force that came from her breasts. After all, given the twenty years age difference, he had the least, if any right to fancy her. Gerry Lord and Leo, unlike their friend Vicky, acknowledged the immense power of sex, thus they could easily forgive Billy, as long as he could keep his urges under control. When he saw that she had been looking at Gerry all along, he smiled at Gerry with relief, and carried on the discussion with a priest's balmy voice.

'You can't blame the whole mankind for that. It's not so simple. In every age-group you can find diverse kind of people, we are not potatoes.'

Choking with laughter and too conscious of Vicki's eyes pinned to his back Gerry stepped up to Lord with a deadly serious face and handed him the letter for forwarding, just to increase the tension. Then he went on stage.

The Apparition

The High-Flyers gave a fine concert and Gerry enjoyed playing. He performed for a girl, who was a lover, a friend. He knew that she was around, he wanted her to be around, he wanted to embalm her with his music, take her to secret places, even to the desert one day. He wanted her, full stop.

Four silly birds were dancing just in front of the band all the time, but Gerry did not play for them. They were drunk and perhaps full of easy, he could not make it out from the stage. Lord used to like it when girls turned on a show, as he said. Gerry thought that in truth he only liked these birds because they were easy to pull, even with Lord's limited skills. Leo at least had some self-respect and he did not take advantage of them. He just smiled at them politely. He was a gentleman; he would never show if he disapproved of someone. Gerry could not stand their swirling, it stirred up his stomach. He, on the other hand, could not stop himself expressing his feelings as often as he could, by spitting on the dry wooden boards of the stage and angrily treading the saliva into the dirt.

When the concert was over Billy immediately started with the disco. Gerry had nothing else to do; he joined the dancers.

After a few tracks he was already swimming in his sweat. His dancing style was so intense; he had to lie down on a few chairs near the door. He was gazing at the wriggling, drunken birds in front of him, getting bored. Then the door opened and two new girls entered whom he had never seen before, a blonde and a redhead. They hovered into the room like the lost children of an unknown civilization, their swinging steps drawing the attention to their tight fitting trousers, which he most enjoyed. They started dancing, in a slower manner than the others did and this excited Gerry even more. He stared at the blonde one and he was magnetized. He felt a tickling excitement in the pit of his stomach and at the roots of his hairs. She was something of a mirage. When the third song started, he moved towards them, by that time he was sure that they were mutually attracted to each other.

Gerry knew that in general terms he was irresistible, especially if he wanted to be, but this girl was different. He was anxious that she might just blow his cover and send him home to his mummy. His trained eyes immediately registered that she was a real blonde and Gerry built a whole structure of sexual philosophy around the blondes and their shades and their effects on men. He knew that he had to stalk this real blonde slowly and cautiously to ensure the perfect effect. His success doped him more: He liked that the game was not easy; there was a challenge to measure his skills.

The music stopped.

'Let's go out for a fag,' he said rudely, for he was embarrassed.

She shook her head.

'I don't smoke.'

'I'd like to get to know you better,' he said almost pleading. Then she nodded and they left the stuffy room to Gerry's unusual relief. Passing the corridor he heard Lord calling after him:

'Bad move, Romeo!' And Leo whistling stupidly in a tone of acknowledgement. He could see from the corners of his eyes Vicky hanging around the door. He suspected that she was waiting for him, for her face lit up when she caught sight of him, but he ignored her, pretending not having noticed. Vicky blushed when she saw the new girl behind Gerry, then she turned green with envy.

Gerry knew what would be Leo's and Lord's next move.

I could be doing the same if I was a jackass, he thought, *chatting up Vicky and using her anger against me for their own benefit.* No sweat! He was the number one with his score; he had no doubt about that.

It was cold and foggy outside. They leaned on the cold wire fence near the entrance and Gerry blew a protective bubble of smoke around them. Under the orange neon street light her face transformed into a pop-art holy Mary: her strong jaws and straight nose built a shape like the cup of a flower, her fluffy hair shining yellow-blue in the darkness, creating a kind of halo around her head.

Even her name was mysterious: Saoirse, the Gaelic word for freedom. Although he did not care for Irish, Gerry knew this one for sure, and when he first heard her name a shiver ran down on his back as if it meant fate. They soon indulged in a chat perforated with long pauses, during which they just looked into each other's eyes lost for words. They talked about the novel: *Angela's Ashes.* She told him that she was seventeen and wanted to study English literature, if possible at Queens. Gerry did not want to seem insolent, so he tried to keep back laughter. He found her use of language too ridiculous. She used the word 'a bit' so often, and with a chirpy cheery emphasis, like a bird, indeed. She might have been embarrassed, too. He imagined that in her world everything must be tiny and tidy. She made him feel that he was in the company of a seventy-year-old spinster.

'What are you laughing at?' she asked him nervously.

'I'm beginning to fall into bits,' he said, adding to himself: *for you.*

'Why?'

'You are bombarding me with a bit all the time,' he imitated her high-pitched voice.

'I use it instead of wee, just in order to be different. My folks are overusing wee, but I think it's the same in Lurgan.'

'In some circles. But where are you from if not from Lurgan?'

'Newry. I'm on a visit here for the weekend.'

'For the wee-kend?'

'Yes, it's wee enough.'

They laughed, and then just gazed at each other.

Meanwhile Gerry was searching in the back of his mind. He did not understand why had this miniature phrase such power that it made him respect her. He found this even more ridiculous. He laughed and then he remembered that his father's mother used a similar belittling word ever so often. She trilled itsy-bitsy with the same tone of voice. By now she was part of the legend that Gerry built from his time in England, but her shining blue eyes smiled back at him from the past. This short trip in time made him laugh out loudly again. The girl in the present was disturbed by his amusement and changed the subject abruptly.

'I heard that your friends called you "Romeo" instead of Gerry. Why?'

'Some people see a connection between Leonardo di Caprio and me. You must have seen him in *Romeo and Juliet*, too.'

It was her turn to burst out laughing.

'Jesus. Does this mean that you are the heroic first time lover in disguise?'

'You better find it out for yourself. But there is another connection: I was a prod, but I stopped going with the gang. I put up a band instead.'

She was suddenly scared, he could see. She quickly put on the mask of the mature lady. She was smiling and nodding like a grandmother. Was she always like this? Perhaps, she just wanted to use her one-year age advantage for self-defense.

'Is the band called the "Capulets"?'

'Ha-ha. No. We are the "High-Flyers."'

This impressed her.

'Where did you get this name from?'

'It was one of those divine inspirations, when the firmament opens and you just know.' He was lying. It was actually Leo's idea.

'Everybody wants to get away from here, that's why.'

'Really? I don't want to get away, but I would like this to be a peaceful and happy place.'

'Isn't that a big ambition, too? I think you are a high-flyer.'

She laughed and her heart visibly opened for a moment.

'What instrument do you play?'

'Didn't you see me playing?'

'No, sorry, I missed it.'

'The drum and most wind instruments,' he said sadly, for he thought he had only played for her during the concert.

'I'm really sorry that I missed your playing,' she said seriously, fully aware of his feelings.

This was what he needed to hear. The grandmother transformed back into a bird and Gerry, in order to show her what a cool gentleman he was, pulled out his mouth organ and began to play some blues obediently. He wanted to go to bed with her. He was blowing his desire into that music, till he could see the same flames dancing in her eyes. Then he pulled her on to him and they dived into the heat.

When he hugged her, he could see in the edges of his eyes Lord floating away with Victoria, holding up his fingers in a V behind her back, showing off to Gerry that he had won the bet. His grin was wider than his face. Gerry waved back to tell him to get lost, for he did not care about money or other mundane struggles at that moment. He was more concerned with his feelings. He kissed her and they broke out of Lurgan and ran away into the blonde deserts of Cairo. He took her for a ride on his Triumph. The sand was spraying under the wheels of the motorbike; the sun was burning their skin. Light blue, orange and many shades of yellow fell like a cascade over them. When they arrived back at the back of the club he pulled her closer, and kissed her nose.

'What did you say your name is?'

'Can't you remember? I'll tell you for the last time: Saoirse.'

'I mean your real name.'

She was confused; she was getting angry, so he kissed the freckles on her nose and announced:

'CC Rider.'

Saoirse blushed slightly and her long eye-lashes flattered for a second like the wings of a butterfly, she must have known that blues by Eric Burdon. He suddenly felt like a man and wanted to show off his power like a grand stud in the movies, and also tried to play down the confusing feelings that he had for her, but when he gave her the name she became his own in a sense. A unique new tenderness was the result of this christening that stirred his soul even more.

They went back into the dance room, where CC's cousin, the redhead Orla, was nervously waiting for them, worried that they would be late going home. They hurried into the street, Orla had ordered a taxi.

A minute later CC disappeared in the depth of the car. The mirage vanished. Gerry was standing there, nailed to the concrete, with an aching, swarming desire in his every limb. This feeling was new to him, it was too intense. Strangely enough, it was still there the following morning, and the next and the next and the next.

CC the Snake

It all started with a funeral. My Great Uncle Lanny died of old age and we went to Lurgan, to pay our respects. We stayed at my Auntie Louise's and Uncle John's. I was glad to see my cousin, Orla, who was one year my junior. We used to have loads of fun together whenever we met. The funeral was on Friday and we all had a quiet evening together. Although we were bound to have a bad conscious for being disrespectful to the dead, Orla and me could hardly wait for the day to pass so that we could run and giggle again. After the usual family lunch on Saturday we all went to church for the evening mass, then the family rushed home again. Auntie Louise used to tell my parents that you could be shot for being a Catholic in Lurgan and we had to be careful which side of the street we went on, or which districts of the town we had to mind. I never understood this about Lurgan; I grew up in Newry, where the streets were safe and the sectarian differences were very rarely and then not so harshly expressed.

It took Orla a long time to persuade Aunt Louise to allow us to go out; although we said that we were going to a friend of hers. We only told her part of the story, the other part, and our planned drop-in at the Saturday night disco remained our secret. Aunt Louise softened just because it was St. Valentine's Day. She allowed us to go, under the condition that we went by taxi, which suited us very well. The night was ours, Orla's and mine, and we were heading to the disco in our carriage like princesses.

It was almost ten when we arrived and we had two hours to us. We cruised around looking for some friends of Orla, and then finally started to dance with them, until a childish, strange boy jumped up to us. He was tall and lean and his glance as if he was watching me from very far. It is not easy to explain this. He watched seriously and with interest, but he seemed to be light-years away from the thing he was watching. Of course, he was a member of the band that they called the 'High-Flyers,' but I was not aware of that, thus I found a much more down-to-earth explanation: He was short-sighted, but too vain to wear his glasses.

Well, he came to dance with us and began to flirt with Orla. He made it obvious, however, that I was the targeted audience of the whole performance. First I found this very degrading towards Orla and really silly towards me, not to mention that the boy seemed to make a fool of himself. The only trouble was that he seemed to be very serious about it, and persevered. His strange behavior occupied my mind, and because I could not figure out why he behaved this way it aroused my interest. I had to find out more about him.

When Orla realized what was happening she seemed more annoyed than confused. I was ready to leave with her, but the boy suddenly stopped his peacock dance around her and began to dance with me. I didn't know what to see in this: shyness or impudence, but my doubts vaporized in the heat of his madness. He was dancing like a dervish, all around me. I didn't know in which direction to look. When I looked at Orla I could see that she was just as perplexed as I was and we started to giggle. Meanwhile, I decided that this was all a kind of provocation and if nothing else, it was fun.

Later when we went out for a walk he turned out to be intelligent to my surprise. His name was Gerry, but I heard a guy calling after him: Romeo. I saw the American version of *Romeo and Juliet*. My friends were in a craze about it for a while, especially because of Leonardo di Caprio. I loved that film, too, but loving Leo? I often thought that I was so much older than my generation. I could never join my friends in their craze for actors or pop-stars and when I saw my teenage girlfriends adoring something or somebody to such an extent I always got suspicious.

In reality, I had intended to confuse him with my questions about his virgin-like name, but he came before me. He said he had been given this name because he had been in a gang of proddy boys before. I had no response to this. He could not know that I was Catholic and that my aunt and uncle lost a son through the fights in the streets of Lurgan. Fear started to creep up my throat, while I felt being attracted to him just as strongly. I was trying to hold the front-line awkwardly, while I saw myself surrendering, falling irresistibly towards some incalculable fate, because I liked him. Then I understood that he was, perhaps, really Romeo.

I never before wanted to make love with someone I just met. I knew that the next morning when I woke up I would feel quite guilty about this, but when he was playing the mouth organ for me there was nothing else. I felt as a snake could feel when the serpent-charmer begins to play and the basket opens.

My father was the principal of a maintained Catholic high school in Newry. I think he was sad that they could not conceive a boy, but I am the first-born daughter and he always had high hopes for me. I went to his school till I was old enough to change for my A-levels. Then my parents decided that I had to have the best preparation for the university, and they sent me to Our Lady's Grammar in Belfast, which is a boarding school.

Our Lady's was a mediaeval building at Stranmillis, near Queen's University. The place itself looked rather cold, although it was beautiful. First I liked that it was particularly well lit and you could smell old books and nuns in the air, but later this changed. I did not mind the smell of old books, they enriched my life, but the smell of old nuns became too heavy on my mind. It was rigid and hard, too clean and soapy, and soon after my arrival at the convent I associated it with the cruelties of life.

After the first days I spent in there I realized that I was a numbered prisoner of Our Lady's. I did not have any spare time for myself; I always had to keep account of what I was doing. The nuns and wardens had loads of problems with me. I asked too many questions, and criticized their disciplinary methods. Honestly, they were seldom right about anything, to my mind. It became a constant fight, and they wanted to convert me at any price. They were trying to bring back a lost sheep to the fold. Added to that, as I had an influence on my fellow sufferers due to my personality, the wardens were inclined to make a precedent out of me. It wasn't pleasant!

Because I joined the convent so late, I was only a short-term visitor and had the advantage of having an uninhibited vision that I gained through my upbringing in the outside world. I could see how disfiguring the whole system worked on the girls. Most of them were deeply insecure, infantile in many ways, especially regarding the other sex, at the same time hungry for life, sex, drugs, anything that would give them the feeling of freedom. They were growing up between the tight walls of the convent like circus children in ancient China, who were put into vases at the age of five and let out after maturation to become ridiculous gnomes for the better amusement of the circus audience.

I must be fair and admit that the nuns had a lot to suffer because of us, too. They pressed the water into their palms, at a loss to understand why it ran out from between their fingers. If the pressure had been weaker, perhaps, we would have been satisfied with the little freedom we had; yet, they gave us nothing at all, making the situation worse for everyone, including themselves. Our need for self-expression was suppressed. We should have been allowed to experience life safely, without running too much risk of hurting ourselves, but this was denied as well. We were confused. All we wanted was to break out, but we did not know where to or what for. Nobody told us how dangerous independence could be if you did not know how to deal with it. Nobody prepared us for the relentless wanderings in the vast deserts of emotions, imaginations, thoughts and feelings. Who could have thought what imprisonment in this labyrinth might mean, and what an endless time you could spend in certain insecurity, in a fear caused by a bad choice, once you took the freedom to make it.

Well, the nuns had no idea about life outside those walls either. They had never made choices in their lives, except the one that made them into nuns. Nevertheless, they knew fear as well as anybody else. Their world was just as much informed by fear, for they were also taught that as children. They simply continued using it as a proven method of discipline, to keep us well in hand, but for us this simple measure equaled the rejection of life.

Nobody should be blamed for being stuck or for being at a certain stage of development. Most people would only acknowledge the validity of this statement if it was meant for them. If it was for somebody else, then it would suddenly become wild territory. You must be brave enough to shift your perception. Once you enter this wild territory, however, you get a free ticket for all the other fantastic worlds. Ultimately, you have to be prepared to look into the eyes of God.

Our teachers were given the burden of being responsible for us, yet they had not grown up for this task themselves. Growing up means to accept full responsibility for your own actions, without using the circumstances as an excuse. How many of us can do that?

I had only one teacher in the convent that did not operate with fear. She was just about ten years older than we were at the grammar school. Sister Jacinta was a teacher of history, and although almost all of us hated history, she helped us to look at the recent time with a critical attitude, she let us find newspapers and photographs from the nineteen seventies and we discussed the events in the class. It was real researching that she taught us.

She was so open-minded that she talked about the sexual revolution which happened in America in the sixties and shortly after in Europe as an event of cultural history and she was a nun! She talked about historical events that were only mentioned in whispers, or distorted by the cloak of Catholic martyrdom. We respected her; she was our heroine, who loved truth above all. She became a legend and we circulated stories about her. Nobody could be sure, but there were whispers about her falling out with the head mistress because of the hostile attitude of teachers towards students and the non-accommodating authority they applied.

Unfortunately, Sister Jacinta was sent to another school after a year of service. She was too much of an oddball for our convent.

Blondes Fatales...

Gerry had never tried his luck with a real blonde before. In this respect, he was a virgin, too. There were not many real blondes around, anyway. According to Gerry's theory, there were two types of blondes. Those, who were born blonde and then their hair got darker, either ginger colored or light brown. He called these the farmer blondes. He did not really regard them as real, and did not have problems in dealing with them, either. The other type had light, almost transparent skin, their whole beings made an untouchable impression. Gerry called them noble blondes for most of them pretended to be heavenly creatures that had come to earth requesting all males to bow down in front of them.

CC made him re-evaluate the theory of the real blonde. She was so different from all. He had to admit that he was thrown from the first moment. She was confident, but in a more convincing way. You could see that she believed what she was saying. There was truth in all what she was doing or saying. She was really there. No doubt. She beamed mature calmness, yet she was a rebel, too. Yes, but against all of her deliberation she was willing to do countless crazy things— with Gerry.

She confused him often, for she seemed fragile and

extremely strong at the same time. He never knew whether he should protect her from himself, or give in to the instincts that told him to destroy her. Or perhaps it was much more to the point that he needed protection?

Gerry stayed in Belfast as often as he could after school and in the evenings. They could see each other for some hours in some courtyards, in front of her college, in a cinema or in a café. The time they were allowed together seemed too short, but sometimes they managed to be really alone in a borrowed flat or room. In such a case they were allowed to do anything. They would eat out of each other's mouth, Gerry would spill jelly on her or smeared butter on her in order to lick it off later. And they laughed so much that it hurt.

When Leo's parents left for a shorter or longer while, he lent his bed to them. Everything felt better there, even just talking. When their skins touched Gerry felt safe. He was sure that he could make up for a bad word or his brutal honesty with tenderness. He felt that he could do anything to her because the fact that she stayed with him to this point proved her trust and love. In bed he was soft and gentle; he could just love.

It was at the beginning of May, in the afternoon. CC put to him the usual question that girls ask when they wish to survey their boyfriend's great and unknown past, trying to make it to their own.

'How old were you when you made love to a girl for the first time?'

'Thirteen, in a tent at an outdoor education centre.'

'And what was it like?'

'The girl was brown, three years older. She told me that I was an undiscovered talent. It was delicious, by the way.'

'Do you always have to boast?'

'Do you always have to be so curious? I began to play the clarinet at that time, too...'

'In a camp?'

'Ha-ha, ha. At the age of twelve. I was an undiscovered talent in this field, too.'

'You said thirteen before.'

'I'm sorry, my mistake. I was twelve when I first went to bed with a girl. Happy now?'

'Is there anything more to show off?'

'My dad died at that time, too, some time before my twelfth birthday. It was a significant year.'

He sighed heavily. Naturally, CC became saddened and began to feel sorry for him. Gerry remained silent, enjoying the effect that the drama of his life created, for the very first time.

They had to face another real life drama that day. When they were about to leave, they bumped into Leo who was waiting for them at the doorstep. He was expecting his grandmother any moment. She arrived promptly and CC went into the kitchen to assist her to make lunch for everybody.

Gerry stayed in the bedroom, for he had taken on the honorable task to clear Leo's mess, and he had the honest intention to carry on with it as long as necessary, even if it took ages. He had to fish out endless sheets of papers with musical notes from under the bed and cupboard. On his way out Leo suggested that he simply dumped them into the paper basket, they were rubbish. Gerry insisted on piling up the sheets on the desk and leaving the pain of selection to Leo.

He was wondering why Leo could find it so difficult to choose between the fantastic and the mediocre, when he came across a bunch of scribbles in his handwriting. First he thought they were lyrics and he felt he had the right to read them. The band was a joint effort, after all. Then he saw that the text was written in prose, it could have been the beginning of a short story. He carried on reading it nevertheless, the sheet seemed to have stuck to his fingers, and he could not take his eyes from the letters. It was an incredibly powerful description of the passionate love that a man could ever feel. Gerry's heart was throbbing, he was excited by the fact that he was reading something forbidden and the contents of the writing were so explicitly sensual that he felt sexually aroused, all over his body.

When Leo entered the room again, Gerry rushed to finish tidying, he was so embarrassed. Leo glared at him with bulging eyes, then at the papers, as if trying to swallow a big ball in his throat.

It was all very strange. Gerry did not know about any girl that Leo was going out with. Although he tried his luck endlessly, he never succeeded with scoring a girl. Of course, he could have imagined the whole encounter with the skin and the eyes in close-up and slithering tongue and sighs and touches, but his desire must have had an object. He knew too well that it was impossible to write something like this without being in love.

He became very curious and decided to watch Leo more closely. He had to find out whom that wonderful being could have been, and see whether she stood the test of fire.

Together

My clarity and the fact that I liked to study often made me look like a fool in the eyes of my friends in the convent. Therefore, they were really surprised when they met Gerry. By then they knew of course that I was madly in love with him. My best friend Cathy was extremely curious to meet him, and Gerry wanted to get a girlfriend for his buddy, Leo or Lord, I was not sure at that point. So we arranged a meeting in our favorite Café Maud's.

We were there first, Cathy and me, taking our seats at a window table.

'This is a good place, from here we can see them first,' said Cathy nervously. She giggled, but then suddenly wiped her eye with the back of her hand, which made a disaster out of her make-up.

'Shoot!' she said. 'Did I mess it up?'

'Completely,' I answered.

'I'll go to the loo and take it all off. I hate make-up, anyway.'

'OK. I'll stay here and wait. Be quick.'

She left me there just when I saw Gerry and Lord getting off a bus on the other side of the road. Gerry was very happy to see me and he was full of jokes, his self was more vibrant than ever. Perhaps, he wanted to show off in front of Lord, I was not sure, but he seemed to be proud of me, too.

We were in the middle of our cokes when Cathy finally returned, her eyes red as if she had been crying. She looked miserable, but Lord was impressed anyway, jumping up from the table when he saw her. It seemed that he was really polite, but I think he was just as nervous as her. Anyway, they liked each other.

I could say less about the reaction of my best friend to my lover Gerry.

Cathy was disappointed:

'What can you love about this crazy, childish boy?' There was no satisfying answer to this question, you really could not think it over logically, but I liked his bravery, his daring. I even loved his grin. For me it was not just ironic, but it was questioning, while teasing and honest.

We had been dating for three months before we made love for the first time. I will never forget that excited expectation preceding it. Gerry's best friend, Leo, told us weeks before that his parents would go on a trip to a conference in Germany and we could use his bedroom. I spent those weeks with endless fantasies of lovemaking and pleasure, but reality surpassed all my dreams, and what I woke up to was wonderful.

Leo lived in Stranmillis, close to Queen's University and not too far from my school. This was an old Protestant area. The people who built those houses must have been very conscious of rank and order. In the desolate street all the houses were elevated, so that the pedestrians had to look up at them. You could impossibly see inside the house through the window and you had to walk up a hill before you could knock on the front door. I thought this was a psychological game to make their owners more powerfully respectable, but it could have had other more practical reasons that I could not figure out. Leo's family lived in an old Victorian house and I have never been inside of a house like theirs before. It had high windows; some of them went to the street, others opened to the inner courtyard, where they had a Peter Pan fountain, and a wild English garden.

We went in through the back door that was overgrown with ivy, and Leo led us up into his bedroom on the first floor. It was a lovely, spacious room with high ceiling, huge desk and cupboards, soft Indian carpets. The sun shone through the huge double winged window on the wide double bed, as if pointing us the way. Leo dropped the front door keys on the bedside table:

'There're the keys. When you leave, just drop them into the letterbox.'

He blew a gallant kiss to me. While going out he mumbled between his teeth:

'Have a good time, birdies.'

'Thank you, Leo,' we mumbled as well, anxiously waiting for the door to slide shut behind him. Then we started to undress each other in a frenzied rush as if our lives were in danger. I felt that I had to be invisible for the world, and by taking off my clothes I could strip away its limits. When I was standing uncovered in front of Gerry, I felt absolutely free of self-consciousness, to my own amazement, for the first time in my life. Then we began to analyze each other's bodies, feeling each and every part. Touching, tasting, caressing with all the care of the world. Slowly, he explored all my sensitive points. I did not move for a while. He did not let me. I was lying there, exposed, vulnerable, but trusting, like a little ant on a human palm. He kissed me all over. I gave in to pleasure. I forgot myself. When he first cautiously entered my being I simply accepted the pain as part of the parcel. It had something mystical about it; first it was hugely shocking and alien, but then suddenly very much my own ancient inherent pain of being a woman. Pain gave way to pleasure and I felt everything more intensely than ever before, as if something had opened my eyes to the wonders of the world again. I was aware of his lean being bordered by white rosy skin as if it had been my realm. I was its queen. If I wanted it was a sea, or a cave, where I could do what I liked and did not have to be afraid of anything. Where I was free. My king, whose realm I was, being naked took off his ironic grin as well. He became innocent but not ignorant because he knew exactly the path to the yet undiscovered heights and depths of my world.

Our love life had to flourish in the shadow of danger all along. Even this first encounter of the deeper skin, my magnificent entry into womanhood was threatened by disturbance, as I would find out later.

Leo had intended to go to the movies while we were dwelling at his place, but on his way down the street he met their neighbor Mrs. Gaghy. She was gardening the front yard.

'Good afternoon, Mrs. Gaghy. How are you?'

'Grand, Leo, what about yourself?'

'I'm well, thank you. I'm going to the cinema.'

Mrs. Gaghy was a caring old lady, who could not imagine how Leo's parents could leave him alone for two weeks in the big house.

'Did your parents phone you last night?'

'Yes, they phone every night. They're very well, thank you.'

'Are you not scared in the evenings? You hear about so many burglaries these days.'

'We have an alarm, Mrs. Gaghy. I always put it on at night.'

'Good boy, you are, Leo.'

'Thank you for being so kind.'

Leo really knew how to speak to other generations and his words usually had an effect. Mrs. Gaghy nodded with understanding:

'It's all right.'

He wanted to rush on when the old lady stopped him again.

'Well, that reminds me. Your grandmother was here this morning. She told me that she was coming back this afternoon to talk to you about the mess. She said it's just like a pigsty in your room.'

Leo came to a sudden stop. He gave up and answered like a sleepwalker.

'Then I'd better go and begin to tidy up.'

He came back into the house. He sat down on the bottom of the stairs, taking care not to disturb us. He curled up in worries, waiting for his grandmother's arrival. Leo guarded the entrance to our heaven like an anxious angel.

The Brutal Truth

In truth, Gerry's father died in 1988, when he was seven. He was working as an electrician and he was electrocuted with 380 volts while at work. He survived with a severe heart injury, but two months later, after an unsuccessful operation in London he died. Everybody did their utmost for him, the whole world, but he gave up. He who was once an SAS hard man, then a spy for the East and West in Cairo, the hero of Gerry's dreams had to die in such a ridiculous way, in a self-imposed accident. This was what Gerry thought with his seven-year-old mind and his pain turned to deep anger. He rose against him and against his world, silently and steadily against all the adults' world. He rose against God.

With the years as he grew freedom became his only ideal. Freedom to do what he wanted, freedom to say what he felt. In many ways, he thought, he was more a rebel than many IRA guys were. As he opened his eyes he felt more and more disgust and contempt for the petty opportunists, mass of cowards, the sheep community that was guarded by fear and hatred. They were frightened of everyone that belonged to any organization with those abbreviated names; nobody was sure who were the goodies or the bad guys in this game. All those letters for terrorist groups spelled out FEAR and a neighbor or a wild stranger alike could have represented it.

On the other hand, the police were brutal and oppressive far from being the defenders of justice. Fear was a measurable medium around; one could slice it and eat it like a piece of bread. People got used to it, just like to the police cordons and the check-ups, the dead had more respect than the living, grief was more familiar than joy, and the only release was talking. Talk as long as you can, tell a story, divert the attention from the here and now, and walk away into the world of words. Tell a tale about the thin desert skies, about the heroic father, the heat and the drought.

As soon as they settled in Lurgan, Gerry started to take over the role of the man in the family. He had developed an opinion that influenced his later attitude towards all females. Experience taught him that he had to be mean to women, and then they would do anything he wanted. From his early years this attitude impregnated his being and he became the embodiment of a nasty habit. What he never understood was the fact that he did this even to the one girl he fell in love with. His mother did not show opposition, she agreed that he had to decide in his own affairs and supported him in everything as far as their humble circumstances allowed. Seamus had no power to change this arrangement, though he did not like it. His attempts only resulted in Gerry's always-scarcer appearances at home, as soon as he was old enough to do so.

Gerry did everything to be different from Seamus, the invader. Inside his head, he always rebelled against the precaution to use his mother's maiden name during their visits to West-Belfast and when he was beaten up for standing up for his own name he felt, he was finally initiated into manhood. That blow into the face transformed him into a Tanner again.

One spring, at the start of the football season he started to support the Glasgow Rangers. He was never really interested in soccer, but that was a different story altogether. He wore blue red and white whenever he could, even under his school uniform. He regularly turned up at the youth club organized by the Presbyterian Church. It was a natural consequence that a Protestant gang of teenagers picked him out. It was not easy to win their trust, though. The guys were suspicious first. He was a stranger. Even worse, he lived in the Catholic area of the town. Most of the boys hated Catholic 'taigs' as they called them, mainly because they had victims of bomb attacks in their families, but mostly they did not need a reason. They grew up in hate. The fact that they accepted him was a great victory over Hector, the leader of the gang, who was the most doubting, always ready with some sarcastic remarks about Gerry's parts of the world.

Gerry, relying on his innate talent of story telling, kept the boys amazed with stories about his father's selection and training and about his life at the SAS.

'My Dad, you know, first had to get through a physical test which meant a long distance hike, and a short distance, but timed, run. For the long distance test, he had to carry about sixty pounds of weight and a rifle. How would you like that? The short distance run was eight miles, but he had to complete this in an hour.'

'Bloody Hell, that's the test,' said a younger boy amazed.

'And that is nothing. In the combat phase, if you were strong enough to pass the physical test, you learn to use weapons and tactics to outwit and outmaneuver enemy forces in the jungle in Africa or Asia. My da did his combat training in the Indian jungle. The SAS is the only regiment that uses live ammunition on their combat phase. This is because they have to learn that they only get one chance.'

'God blame me. That's for real?'

'Yeah, but hear what was the third test. After the combat he had to go through survival and escape and evasion training. In this phase candidates that are left from the hundreds that apply will undergo a survival phase in the jungle, in which they only have a small survival kit.'

'What's tha'?' shrieked one of the boys called Jerome, and Gerry was pleased to see some excitement even in Hector's eyes.

'Water resistant tin, vinyl tape, button compass, knife, matches, pencil, purification tablets, snare wire, candle, flint and striker, hacksaw blade, fishing kit, whistle, sewing kit, safety pins, wire saw,' Gerry recited the list from his memory, which he had taken from the internet the night before.

'Wow. Wire saw! Sounds cool,' said Jerome again, and another boy added: 'Yeah, I saw one of those in *Rambo*; they roll it around their finger just and...' He jumped up and pretended to cut through Jerome's throat.

'He had to "survive" for a week while evading an enemy tracking party. This is a particularly hard phase because the tracking party is normally accustomed to the ground. After this week, he had to give himself up at an agreed meeting point. Then he was taken back to the enemy headquarters and interrogated.'

'What? By his own people?'

'He did not know them, but yeah, in principle his own people. This would make or break any candidate's career as they must undergo physical and mental torture as well as aggressive interrogation. That's two in a hundred, man.'

So, Gerry's place in the gang was established, next to Hector's if not even usurping it. They respected him, or better to say, they respected the huge shadow of his dead father.

The gang hung around at nights mostly, they drunk beer and threw stones into shop windows when they felt like it. Hector had a criminal history for vandalism and beatings and he had been in a juvenile prison for a short time. He knew how to make Molotov cocktails and they practiced throwing them on an open field. As the marching season approached, July became their peak time; everything was building up to the eleventh and the twelfth. They did not know why, but their rage rose with every day and they left a bloodline of burning cars and buses around the town.

Gerry later realized that joining the prod gang was his last desperate attempt to identify with his dead father. He was seriously thinking of getting a tattoo of the winged dagger on his right shoulder, to be marked forever by his heroic past. He did not have enough experience to know that desperate beginnings were inevitably leading to tragedies.

One night they came across one of Gerry's neighbor's kids Fergus in a street fight. He popped up in front of them with his friends, all wearing black and red shawls, the colors of the Celtic. They were all younger than their opponents, Fergus was only eleven, and Gerry knew that for sure. When the young Catholics saw the proddies' advantage in numbers and years, they ran away. Fergus only stayed because he saw Gerry and his sight stunned him. He knew Gerry too well; Gerry had used to play soccer with his brothers Peter and John when he was younger. Hector grabbed Fergus' throat and was ready to knock him down when Gerry intervened, yelling:

'Hang on! I know him, he's all right.'

Hector stopped and looked at Gerry suspiciously.

'So. You're defending a taig.'

The silence that followed filled with electricity, the air pulsated anxiety, and Gerry knew the thunder would hit him in a second. The gang members turned towards him surprised, with growing hostility. Hector's face lit up by his own idea of fun.

'Gerry, choose, now or never. You've to whack him in front of us.'

They circled Gerry and Fergus in and Gerry had to face the terror in the young boy's eyes. It became a messy business. Gerry took Hector. The rest of them, about six lads in heavy boots and leather gloves started to kick and fist Fergus and

Gerry where they could reach them. There was a moment when Gerry wished he had never been born. He fought with all his anger, but he felt most anxious for Fergus, who fell on the ground after one of the brutes kicked into the pit of his stomach. This was the moment, when Gerry pulled the jack-knife out of his back pocket. A brief pause followed that gave Fergus the opportunity to get up and run.

The next thing Gerry heard was the alien sound of a thump and following that the squeaking breaks of a car. The next thing he saw was Fergus falling from the air and rolling on the concrete towards him. The gang spread immediately. A sudden silence surrounded him and Fergus, who was lying on his back, staring at the sky. His body looked like a bundle of red lumps, his limbs visibly softened and twisted.

Gerry collapsed on Fergus' body, but his aching fingers could not feel the pulse in his neck. The alarming fear gave him a huge surge of energy, he jumped up and ran to the car, opened the door and tore the mobile from the driver's trembling hands who was trying to call 999, but could not utter more than a mumble with his stony tongue. Deep down Gerry already knew that Fergus was dead, but it was necessary to do something, to pretend that there was something he could do. The driver seemed to be on the brink of death himself; he definitely needed some treatment. Gerry felt the blood getting firm on his chin and under his left ear.

Finally, the ambulance and the police arrived, but it was too late for Fergus. Gerry had to witness. He did not know surnames; he could only give a description of the gang members. He did not see any need to cover for the gang, and they really were not his friends. He told the police that he had been together with Fergus when the gang attacked them, with a faint attempt to make things look softer in the eyes of his conscience. The police sent him home.

From this time on he became the whackers' target, too. His life became a terrible chaos. He spent the summer in fear, virtually feeling death's cold breath in his neck. Nobody could have hindered a punishment rage against him and the police warned him to be very careful. Considering that he was only fifteen this was hell on earth. Although he managed to hide in Belfast or Bangor from the brutalos, he could not run away from the guilt that plagued him.

There was another lost person in his life to grieve for and he cried for Fergus as he did for his father. One of the few real memories he had from his father became more vivid than ever before. The night when he finished his service at the army, Gerry heard him telling his mother how happy he was to be a civilian again. Gerry was about three, very small, but he remembered that night clearly, for his father bought him a tricycle that day to make it more memorable. Barry took his wife and child into his arms and said:

'No more fighting,' and they all laughed.

This memory presented itself like a message from father to son to burn Gerry's soul and face. He realized that he had not been acting in the name of his father as his original desire had been; in fact he brought shame to his father's memory. Yes, his father fought terrorism, but Gerry's rowdy outbursts were only the ridiculous pantomime of the just fight. In reality, they served as an outlet for his anger about losing his dad, and to his shame and deepest humiliation they were directed against innocent people. The image of Fergus' lifeless body lying on the road haunted him the whole summer. He felt guilty whenever he saw Fergus' mother. Her gestures slowed down by the weight of her pain, her whole stature looked as if half of it had been torn away.

It was a relief to start school in the autumn after this incident, when he could hide camouflaged in his school uniform, commuting from Lurgan to Belfast. He dived into his music and repaired the old motorbike. He finished it by his sixteen's birthday. Ma gave him his dad's leather overall as a present that she had kept as a memory. Gerry realized that his real inheritance from his father was the love of the motorbike, and contrary to his mother's fears it often saved his life. On the back of his Triumph he was able to get away from places when the situation became too threatening.

Synchronicity

Into their first seven months Gerry did not take CC seriously enough. He was merely enjoying the game.

Lord inspired the idea of the GAME, though he did not know about it.

Lord was not only his friend, but acted as a business agent for him on occasions, helping Gerry to sell poems, songs, anything he was capable to create. As time went on, Gerry felt more and more exploited by him. Lord had the annoying habit of abusing his power, as a friend and as a business agent alike. He wanted to know more and more private details about his relationships, especially about his latest score: CC. In the past, before CC, Gerry often used Lord's curiosity to enhance their shared business success, giving him a few scraps of information about his sex life, but only as much as necessary. He could be sure that Lord circulated them, and the implicit image of the macho hero helped to keep the schoolmates' interest alive, so that they kept coming back for the goods, especially the love poems. They sold really well.

Since he had become involved with CC, however, he was uncharacteristically secretive, for he himself was a bit perplexed. He was trying to make Lord believe that this relationship was something mysteriously incomprehensible for him so that he stopped bothering him with indiscreet questions.

They were coming out of school one day. Gerry slowed down to hang around the gate, waiting for CC, who was, as he hoped, due to arrive within minutes. It seemed like a miracle that she was able to come to his school that afternoon. Being Friday, they had agreed that they would spend a couple of hours together before she would catch the last train to Newry. Luckily, his school was very close to the railway station, which made their plan look easier. It was a gamble to know whether CC had been given permission to leave school after lunch and Gerry would only find out when he saw her. Lord stuck with him, smelling some new gossip. After a second he started:

'Tell me, how can you keep this relationship intact with CC? She's either in Belfast or in Newry, you in between in Lurgan. When do you meet? You must spend a fortune on phone calls.'

'I don't have to know that I'm meeting her,' Gerry said as a matter of fact. He could see the rising amazement on Lord's face, which ignited his imagination.

'Don't you have dates?'

'We've agreed not to fix anything. We just meet accidentally.'

'Are you a freak? Someone'll snatch your baby, man!'

Gerry found it impossible to keep back a grin looking at Lord's perplexed face, but then he put on his instructor mask and went on:

'It's not so easy to steal her, brother. I know where she is now better than she knows herself. This is a kind of telepathy, my sweet Lord. Haven't you heard about it?'

Gerry actually was reading about synchronicity at that time and he found it fascinating. He could be sure, on the other hand, that his good old friend did not know about Carl

Gustav Jung, and his theories. In Gerry's eyes Lord was a man of the masses in many ways and he wanted to stay over the surface. Gerry was quite sure that Lord never stuck up for him when the doubting Thomases grinned behind his back and questioned the stories of his early years in Cairo and his SAS man spy father. Although Lord liked to listen to these stories, like everybody else, he silently gave his agreement that Gerry was a compulsive liar, a jerk, whatsoever, just to save his own ass and not to seem crazy.

In this instance, Lord soon resigned himself to his chicken philosophy that used to make Gerry furious.

'That's psycho. If you have a date, you'll be able to keep to it, and you can be sure she'll be there for you.'

'That's what I don't need at all,' Gerry replied plainly, but something must have snapped in Lord's brain. Assuming that he was in a superior position he asked for evidence:

'Where is she now then?

'OK,' Gerry gave in generously. 'If you need something to wonder at, my friend. Just watch! She'll appear around the corner in a minute.'

When Lord looked towards the end of the crescent, he could see cars and trucks passing on the main road, but there was only an old woman wobbling about, leashed to her dog. He grinned at Gerry victoriously, flashing his teeth like a jackal. Gerry checked the time: forty seconds left from the minute. Lord imitated his stolen glimpse at the watch, but he transformed it into an amateurish pantomime.

When Gerry raised his head he knew he was lucky again. At the end of the street, the glorious blonde appeared. He smiled and watched Lord's face turning into stone. CC seemed to be at a loss for a moment, checking whether she was in the right street. Her apparent confusion fitted into Gerry's show perfectly. Then he whistled and waved to her.

She waved back to them. Lord turned towards Gerry

angrily, trying to cover his confusion from CC—just to be confronted by the broad grin on Gerry's face. He accused Gerry almost choking on his own words:

'You want to make a barmy out of me again!'

'Oh boy, you're really skeptical! But you know what: you should ask her.'

He wanted to grant him a chance in this uneven game, but Lord chickened out, just as Gerry had assumed.

'No way. I don't want her to think that I'm mad. I want your baby to like me. She might fancy me when you got sick of her.'

'The big coward you are, you're trying to hit me under the belt,' Gerry was still hiding his feelings,

'But for the time being: I don't think so.'

Lord hit back again:

'I'll only give you a few weeks more. I know you.'

The traffic light at the nearest corner signaled green and CC finally crossed the road. She looked in her usual clear way at them, unsuspecting, though very much in her power. Gerry did not know where all this power was coming from. He would find it out later, almost too late: Her personality was interwoven with trust and faith.

She arrived, and gave Gerry a kiss:

'Hi, you two. How are you, Lord?'

Lord leaned over to her and kissed her left cheek with delight:

'Everything is OK, now that I've seen you, but I have to go, my instrument is calling me and so are the cracked neighbors. I can't wait to chase them out of the world with my trumpet. Bye!'

He left totally transformed like a new person; so that Gerry immediately became suspicious of him, jealously thinking that he had a crush on Saoirse.

Thanks to this intercourse with Lord, the idea of

synchronicity gained momentum in his mind and excited him more than ever.

'Let's go to the café, CC, I have to talk to you.'

'All right, but I can't pay for both of us this time.'

'That's dead on. I'm Mr. Rich today.'

She just looked at him unbelieving, with a naughty smile on her face. He had to show her the fiver that he borrowed from an infatuated bird at school that day.

'Where is it from?'

'Judy and Debbie threw it at me. They love me, you see. I'm so irresistible, nobody can refuse me.'

She laughed, taking his statement for a joke. Laughter was always a good sign as far as Gerry was concerned, but it embarrassed him this time as he was seriously trying to impress her.

In the café, they were sitting at the window, drinking the Coke that Gerry had to work so hard for. He asked Saoirse to join him in his new madness:

'CC, I'd like to talk about something serious now! I've been reading about Carl Jung's work. He was a psychiatrist, and his main idea was that there is a collective unconscious, which is like the ocean underneath all thought. We are all part of it and we are all connected through it. This is the possible explanation for things like telepathy.'

She frowned. Gerry was open to her skepticism, yet he carried on, he was on fire.

'It came to my mind when you arrived to the school. Even if you have doubts about it, let's make an experiment! We won't have any dates in future. We'll meet by intuition only. What do you think?'

She was caressing her glass slowly and methodically, as if she wanted to get between the molecules:

'You mean that we say good-bye now and we don't have the slightest idea about when or where we meet next?'

'Exactly. That's it. That's the fun of it, you know! That we won't know where the other one will be. We should feel it and then we'll be able to find each other. I'm quite sure that I would find you,' he said and he really meant it.

'It'll be exciting.' She blew out through her perched lips as if the mere idea exhausted her already. It all seemed like a hard job to her. She had to contemplate it for a little while. She was searching for a sensible way out, but then she saw that he was losing his patience.

'If you promise, I'll agree,' she said quickly to stop him becoming deflated.

'I promise, but you have to do something, too.'

'You mean I'll have to think of you a lot.' She spread out her enigmatic smile.

'Only if you really want me to be with you.'

'Well, I'll see. If I really want to be with you.' She paused. 'Is this a test?'

Gerry shrugged his shoulders, for he did not want to give away himself. She smiled skeptically. For a second he had doubts himself. It had little accord with their ideals of freedom, if he wanted to fill up her being and even control her thoughts, but the game felt fine to him and gave him and their relationship a new drive.

That afternoon they made a first attempt just to prove to themselves that the whole thing was going to be a piece of cake.

They said good-bye. Gerry played the fool when he got on the motorbike, in order to coax a smile on her worried face. Then he left. The next corner he stopped smoked a cigarette and gave her time to go somewhere, and change position. Then he turned back and followed her usual route towards the railway station. He found her sitting on the steps of the Presbyterian Church in the sunshine. She was reading. He got off his bike and sneaked closer to her and she did not notice him. Then he stood over her, casting a shadow on her book.

This was not the sort of surprise Northern Irish people liked, especially not in Belfast. The ghosts of the past, the killings and beatings in the streets were still there, lurking around, haunting them, and sometimes reappearing with all their power, just when they would start to feel that they had changed their world. Gerry was dancing on the thin rope between fear and love. She was not naïve. For a second Gerry could feel the shocked trembling in her. This feeling of terror was jeopardizing the success of the whole game and he knew that if it was necessary, he would have to give it all up in order to save CC's sanity. Suddenly, he felt immensely powerful and tender at the same time.

Looking at his feet, she recognized him from his shoes. She smiled at them. Gerry sat down close to her thin body and took her into his arms.

'Have you called me?'

As an answer, CC laughed. Gerry took out his instrument and played for her. This was his way of transforming emotions, the most beautiful way of hiding them. He was brimming with exhilarating joy.

In the next minute a pound coin fell into the open case of the clarinet and it seemed like a response of the gods, meaning that his idea would pay off. On the other hand, being practical and having firm roots in reality, Gerry had just discovered a new way of earning money. Practicing in the street and being paid for it was more than he could have asked for.

It was not easy for them to start the synchronicity game. Gerry was very excited and wanted to experience the power of the mind, but mainly the power of the heart. CC, being the more impulsive lover of the two, often blocked it with her fears. She was seeking the company of his friends in order to find him, too much controlled by her mind.

After many late afternoons spent with aimless wanderings in the city, Gerry found her in the botanical gardens towards evening one day. Cathy, Lord, Leo were there, too. She was sitting on a stone barrier a bit further away from the others, with Leo, immersed in an intense discussion. In a flash of a moment Gerry remembered Leo's passionate piece of writing and he turned his face away. When he composed himself, he still found it safer to remain at a distance. He waved to them to say 'hello.' Against his expectations, she did not immediately come to him and when she did, it was, as he felt it, too late. She approached him in her grandmotherly manner what made him even more furious.

'Hello, how are you, young master?'

'Fine, Grandma.'

'Are you angry with me?' she asked innocently, questioning the obvious.

'Yes, I had to wait one week to see you and you haven't even bothered to look at me when I arrived.'

'You arrived after me. It was your job to come and greet me.'

'There are no jobs in this business. Anyway, I didn't want to disturb you.' This was the truth as Gerry saw it at that moment, but it made CC very angry.

'Really? Well, then don't disturb me now, right?'

Gerry turned round and left, he was extremely disappointed. He felt let down, even abandoned. Leo ran after him:

'Stop fooling about, come back! Nothing's happened; we just had a chat.'

'You've got no idea what this is all about! That chick's completely crazy.'

'But she loves you.' Leo's naivety poured oil on the flames.

'She does love me! Do you know how many girls loved me? Love! The word itself turns my stomach.'

He walked away in fury. He really felt nauseous and was so hurt that he had to thump his soles into the earth, to drive the pain down into his feet. When he was sure that he got out of their sight he stopped, and watched them secretly from behind a tree.

What he saw shocked him. CC was sitting on a big bulk of a stone, her arms hanging down while she was fiddling with her shoelaces. While her body seemed to have a task to perform, her face was dead; she was looking with empty eyes, too sad for him to bear. Now his sulky anger turned into shame, driving him away. He quickly turned his back on the scene and ran.

He wrote a letter to her. He asked her to listen to him inside and not to look for him outside. He knew her to be intelligent and sensitive; therefore he was quite certain that anything could be possible with her. And finally it happened! They bumped into each other one day. Their joy was hilarious! They were standing there in a trance for the first few minutes. Then they kissed and hugged almost hysterically like the reunited victims after a catastrophe, but in their case it was the joy of victory. They achieved something together that most people would regard as insane or impossible, to say the least. For Gerry this was his Orgasm Total. He later wrote a song about it which became number one in the charts and was played constantly on the local FM radio station. For CC this was meta-erotica, some undeserved bliss that was more spiritual, than the pleasure of the flesh.

For the next months this became their frequent game: they did not agree to meet, or fixed a time or place and they were not allowed to look for each other. When their thoughts took them to the most impossible place then the other one had to be there, too. Therefore it happened that Gerry found CC in Belfast Zoo talking to a lion, and once she was waiting for him on the quays at the harbor, perching on top of a bag of cement. Funnily enough water lay between them; Gerry arrived to the quay on the opposite side.

It was always an incredibly great achievement to be there

where the other wished them to be, also because CC was staying in the convent—locked up—as Gerry thought: Her friends often helped her to sneak out, passing the doorkeeper's lodge. The old fatty was mostly eavesdropping to some conversations on the phone; therefore he did not pay attention. The girls walked through the dark corridor on tiptoes. When they peeped into the lodge they could see the doorkeeper, with the telephone in one hand. His other hand was mostly in his pocket, absent-mindedly playing with his penis. He did not say a word, he was just overhearing the conversation, sighing deeply and grinning with delight. When CC shut the heavy main entrance door behind her, Billy looked up scared, but he could only see Cathy or Sylvia scolding him with her index finger. Then the innocent girl put the same sexy finger on her mouth as a warning for Billy, to keep quite. The old man blushed and the bargain was done. Then the girl kept on waving and left him, blowing kisses.

They often met in the library. They were overfilled with the wish to see the other so much that they chose the most probable place. Of course, they broke the rules of the game when they did so, but they accepted these side-tracks as short breaks. The library became an oasis in the city desert where the exhausted travelers could replenish their cups of love. They fell into each other's arms happily and broke into tears.

Gerry was not aware of the significance of these meetings at the time. He was only surprised how he could stand the same girl for so long.

Trust

In the first seven months of ours I loved Gerry blindly, without reservation. I played the game he called synchronicity. This game was the most important experience of my seventeen years old life, I thought, but for almost everybody else, even for my closest friends, it equaled sheer insanity.

We did not agree where or when we would meet, we just called each other deep inside and he would often lead me to dangerous places.

Outside Our Lady's, in the wild and often-dangerous city of Belfast I felt more relaxed, sometimes even free. In the streets I could feel Gerry's calling inside me much stronger. It started from deep in my stomach. In fact, it was a very sexual sensation. It was as if we were drawn together by invisible threads.

Once in the afternoon, I heard Gerry's call. There was no doubt in my mind: I had to go and find him immediately. My mates' arguing was transformed into an incomprehensible and pointless flood of noise in the background. I became the witness, the indifferent viewer. The free part of me—which I called my soul—was already with Gerry, my body lingering about, waiting for the moment when it could escape and join that much bigger reality.

Sylvia was pottering around in the mass of her clothes that she laid out to cover the coldness of her grey metallic bed. This inventory was her every day pleasure, looking at her clothes and imagining herself at some flashy party:

'I'll go and wash my things.'

For some reason, anything she did or said provoked Cathy to make some ironic remarks. There was always a hint of tension in their chats; Cathy had no tolerance for any of her pastimes:

'Honestly, this girl is a maniac, she is so clean! Why don't you sweep up the whole mess in your pretty head at last? That's what you really need.'

'How else am I supposed to spend my time in this convent? Have you got any better idea? I can't write letters all the time. I could always text him if I wanted to see him. If I wrote a letter to him, he would think I was ill. Or maybe that I want to break up with him, but of course, I don't want to do that. He would demolish this convent in his rage.'

'It's high time somebody did that. And what about our friend, Hughie?'

'Nothing at all. What do you mean?'

I needed Cathy's help, therefore I interrupted them:

'I'll try to sneak out.'

Cathy thought it was a bright idea, but when I told her that I wanted to go without her she asked me skeptically:

'One of your unexpected meetings? I really think it is a nightmare. How can you allow him, to invade your mind? You just go where he wants you like a puppet without any will of your own.'

'It isn't like that at all. I just leave a line free for him so that he can contact me. I'm always open for him. It's a wonderful feeling, Cathy. I think, you are jealous.'

'No, I rather believe that you should be more careful whom you open yourself to, but I'll go with you to the Billy's lodge, and I'll distract his attention, if it's at all necessary. I'll always help you, you know that very well.'

There was common sense in her suspicions. Gerry had the air of a macho heartbreaker, but I knew and could really understand why girls loved him. After all, he provoked everyone regardless of sex. You could hate him or love him; there was no middle way. Needless to say, boys came into the first group with a few exceptions, and girls into the second one.

Cathy helped me to sneak out. I was rushing to get into the library before the end of the opening hours. Just when I got in, I bumped into Leo who was on his way out. He stopped me and held me for a moment, searching in my eyes through his thick glasses. I felt like an ant under the magnifying glass, desperate to move on to follow my instincts, to do my task. It felt as if Leo was looking into me. He answered saving me from having to ask the question:

'He's in, don't worry.'

I gave him a kiss on the cheek, muttering something like a 'thank you.'

I found Gerry in the reading section. He obviously missed me too badly. I could sense that he felt like hiding or running away. He whispered into my ears:

'Let's go,' and I knew that Leo's place was free. We were inseparable for the whole afternoon. After having spent a few hours at Leo's, we went to the cinema, but I have no recollection of what we saw. I was so much embalmed in our echoing emotions that I could hardly take in anything else. Love became a physical feeling, heavy and strong, in the humming in my veins, flooding me over. When the film was over we embarked on a soundless walk in the yellow lights of the city. We did not have to talk; we were one without communication. I felt safe, as if we were protected, gliding on the waves of air inside a bubble.

I was late going back to the hostel; Sister O'Hara herself opened the front door for me ten minutes after eleven. She did not say a word, but my blood froze the minute I saw her. I stumbled into my bed in my clothes, wearing him around me, feeling terribly vulnerable and open, feeling an incredible pain without him, my whole body like a wound. For me, this was the afternoon when I really lost my virginity, although physically it happened weeks before. It was so much beyond expectation, painful, yet beautiful and empowering. It took me days to grasp what happened and I never managed to fully understand it, it was so strange.

Be Warned

Sister O'Hara paid special attention to my fostering, and she visited me soon after the night out with Gerry.

We were in our three-bed-room, waiting for her arrival, nervously not daring to do anything that could have been regarded as undisciplined. She had notified us previously in the dining hall that she would come to our room. This was one of her most annoying habits, as if she wanted to keep her remote grip on us, to keep our fearful expectation alive.

Sylvia was pottering among her things. I knew that she was searching for some excuse to leave the room, as she was allergic to the physical presence of Sister O'Hara. Her skin broke out with itchy blisters soon after she had talked to our chief nun, what made us laugh at the beginning. Later, she did not like to talk about it to anybody, not even to us. It was like a handicap. Being anorexic or bulimic was almost a must in some girls' circles, but itchy blisters were too anarchic, too psycho and let's admit, too ugly and contagious. Once you saw her scratching herself you had to do it soon yourself.

In order to avoid Sister O'Hara, and to hide her strange compulsory behavior she used to make up some kind of excuse, this time, playing it very naturally, she said:

'I'd better go and wash my hair before our Lady arrives.'

I had to admonish her, imitating the high-pitched tone of 'our Lady':

'You know, you're not allowed to go and wash your hair during Silencium, my dear.'

'Exactly! That's why I'm going. Try to hold on without me for a while, right?'

Cathy always teased her:

'We'll try. What are you learning, Saoirse?'

'Does it matter?'

'OK. History.'

Sylvia left the room and a moment later Sister O'Hara appeared in her black gown and white head-dress. She chattered her dreadfully boring repetitive question on entering:

'What are you learning, girls?' She never assumed that we could do anything else.

We replied in a choir: 'History.'

Sister O'Hara expressed her satisfaction:

'I'm very pleased to hear this. It's good to go over your lessons again, especially because the final exams are approaching. Saoirse, you want to become a teacher so it's especially important for you.'

'Yes, Sister O'Hara.'

'But I don't want to talk to you about this. It's about your absences from the hostel. You have been seen with a boy.'

'Pardon?'

'I only want to say that you shouldn't cross your bridges until you come to them.'

'Pardon?'

'I mean, you shouldn't get deeply involved in situations which could end badly.'

'Sorry?'

'Something which seems important now, perhaps won't be in the future.'

'I'm sorry; I don't know what you mean!'

I swallowed my anger. I was lying. Of course, I knew what she meant. I had to think of the ridiculous sexual education we were getting, the 'How to not to' as we used to call it. Don't have sex before marriage, don't use contraception, and don't have abortion. The sins our pope imposed upon us by denying our bodies' love. If the only reason for sex was procreation, how could it be so powerful? Did God really want the world to be overpopulated? So that war and epidemics would be the only answer for a quick cleaning up? I regretted my anger immediately and determined to listen to her with my left ear and let everything flow out through my right ear. She still did not notice how superfluous her concerns were.

'Well, how shall I say it? There is only one true love in everybody's life, Saoirse, and this isn't a true love for you.'

'How do you know?' I asked, again losing my temper. However, her reply proved that the discussion was pointless as she was just blathering something she never believed herself.

'I know you: you're a serious girl. Be careful with your reputation! Don't waste it!'

I instantly had to think of her reputation. There was an unbelievably cheeky gossip in circulation about our chief warden. Billy, the doorkeeper of the convent, had overheard some mysterious phone calls. Many of us saw him listening to conversations. He found utmost pleasure in them, so much that he often forgot to attend his job of watching the entrance. Once Valerie, the caretaker's daughter, checked the matter. When she saw Billy enmeshed in eavesdropping she ran to the workshop in the basement, picked up the phone and heard Sister O'Hara courting an ominous man at the other end of the phone, who seemed to be somebody important in the ministry's educational department. After this everybody wanted to know that Sister O'Hara had a lover.

'Pardon?'

'I'm really very concerned about you. You're a talented girl and you shouldn't forget your aim in life. This boy would only spoil your purity, and for what?'

'Yes, Sister. I'll remember that.' This seemed to satisfy her.

'Girls, if you have any problems that you want to discuss in private, you know you can always count on me.'

This was more than we could bear. She would have been the last person to divulge our secrets to. When she finally slipped though the door, leaving behind the strong smell of cheap soap we burst out laughing like crazy.

'Isn't she like a bad commercial? You know that you won't buy what she is selling, even if she killed you,' said Cathy between gurgles.

When Sylvia arrived we had to tell the story again, by which time we had worked out a scenario for a TV commercial in which Sister O'Hara would bite into the soap and start talking in bubbles. The bubbles would be drawn like in the comics, and each bubble would contain her real thoughts. Like sitting in a rowboat with the mysterious stranger, and kissing passionately under the head-dress.

Friends

I was the sensible, thoughtful one in the group. It might sound boring, but I never liked adventures of the common type. I did not go out to come back drunk after an hour and did not pick up a new guy every day. On the other hand, although I was not a companion in their escapades, my friends could always rely on me. They could tell me everything; I was a good listener and a good comforter. Besides all these I was prepared to keep my back there for the whole gang if it was necessary.

Once I was sitting and learning a sonnet by Shakespeare, when Sylvia dashed into the room. She could hardly stand on her feet, she was crying blind drunk. Cathy followed her, tipsy as well.

Sylvia fell on the bed and Cathy told me the story:

'This crazy girl picked up a guy in the pub, who was all muscles and brawn.'

'Not so loud! The whole hostel will hear everything.'

She carried on with lower voice, but still gasping for air:

'OK. He bought us a couple of drinks, and he tried to persuade Sylvia to go up to his flat, and this mad chicken wanted to go almost immediately. I had to hold her back. When he tried to knock me down, she suddenly realized it wasn't such a good idea. Our little Sylvie began to boohoo and scream. We had to run back to the hostel on our soft legs like two rag dolls, and we had to creep on all fours in front of the doorman's lodge, you can imagine what it was like.'

Sylvia was devastated and hysterical. She thought that she had betrayed her boyfriend:

'Robbie will hear about it, won't he? That I have betrayed him.'

I had to quieten her; a warden could have come in at any moment. We held her head under the tap over the washbasin that was in the farthest corner of our room. She calmed down slowly.

I felt so sorry for her. She was under shock. She obviously had never assumed that alcohol could make her give up all her priorities so quickly. Her own irresponsible willingness to go with a man just like that scared her immensely. I knew that drugs could turn a person inside out and upside down, but it was impossible for me to explain this to her at that moment in time, so I just assured her:

'He won't know anything about it. Don't be afraid, nobody will tell him.'

We laid her down on the bed, she was still grumbling and blabbing when without warning, like a dark shadow, Sister O'Hara entered the room.

'What are you learning, girls?' she asked her usual question.

Suddenly cold sober, Cathy sprung in front of Sylvia's bed, to cover her up. Sister O'Hara looked at her examining the distorted features of her face. She opened her mouth to ask something, when I interfered, moving towards her:

'Sister O'Hara, could I talk to you privately, please.'

Sister O'Hara was still glaring at Cathy, so I added hastily:

'About a very private matter?'

'Of course, Saoirse. You know that I am here for you.'

She looked at me half suspecting, half-happy.

'What do you want to talk about?'

'Matters of love,' I said boldly. The blood stopped in my veins while I was watching the old nun's face blooming, enveloped in a sparkling mist.

'Come up with me to my room, Saoirse; let us leave Cathy alone to learn her English in peace. But of course, without any music, Cathy. How many times have I told you girls that you can't concentrate while you are listening to music?'

I switched off the radio and followed Sister O'Hara to her room. I had a few minutes to invent some important issue to talk about. The subject ought to be not too personal, but neither too banal to keep her satisfied. When we arrived in her room I offered her:

'Sister O'Hara, I would like to read a love poem by Yeats at the prize giving ceremony, please.'

'That's an unusual request. Why a love poem?'

'The prize giving is exactly on the day of my parents' wedding anniversary and I would like to present them with that.'

'Hm. Which one you mean?'

I was on fire. My favorite poem by Yeats was 'He wishes for the Cloths of Heaven' and I actually knew it by heart:

'Had I the heavens' embroidered cloths,
Inwrought with golden and silver light,
The blue and the dim and the dark cloths
Of night and light and the half-light,
I would spread the cloths under your feet:
But I, being poor, have only my dreams;
I have spread my dreams under your feet;
Thread softly because you tread on my dreams.'

Even Sister O'Hara seemed a bit softened by the melody of these words. She smiled at me benevolently.

'Beautiful. You can cite it; of course, you are very good at it indeed. I think, though that the purpose of this present should remain our secret. You can of course, tell your parents privately. It is a lovely idea.'

Just when I was leaving, she called after me:

'Since you joined our school I have always thought that your greatest love should be literature, Saoirse. I'm very pleased that I was right.'

I felt immensely relieved that I managed to save Sylvia from detention or perhaps from being suspended, but I was evenly cross with her. I spent the next couple of days listening to her apologies. Cathy did not talk to her for about two days, either, but in fact she was just as guilty in this instance. I really felt fed up with their energy wasting childishness.

Face-Painting

My father sensed the enemy in Gerry instinctively. Dad hated Gerry from the minute I spoke out his name for the very first time, without having ever seen him. At their first and last meeting, my father's underlying prejudice was tactile in the air, but I must admit, Gerry did not try to smuggle himself into my old man's heart either.

One summer evening, just one week after I had finished my summer exams, we traveled on Gerry's motorbike to Newry. I enjoyed the speed; we were gliding along the road in the sunshine.

Unexpectedly, Gerry stopped at a desolate forest belt.

We got off the bike and he smiled at me mysteriously, taking my hand. I was a bit scared and excited at the same time:

'What? Oh my God. Do you want to make love here?'

'Yes, yes!'

'And you don't care how I feel about it?'

'You'll love it, I know.'

He was right. We kissed and I forgot where we were, I was one with him, with the green meadow and the grey-blue sky. Raindrops woke us with smooth monotonous stitches on the face, and we had to make the last part of the journey in sizzling rain.

When we arrived to my parents' house I was still drunk with love. My unusual happiness was striking for my mother. She sensed some unevenness, some invisible crease on the whitewashed surface of my official virginity, but she chased away the thought for she was scared, even by the assumption that her daughter could do something that did not align with the morals she had professed.

When I hugged her I had a vague memory of her big and soft breasts, and the gap between them. She had breast fed me until I was about two and I had been allowed to insert my index finger into this gap, playing an innocently exciting game as if I had been looking for food in there. She had turned a blind eye to this somewhat forbidden game. She let me play it when we were in underwear together, on rare occasions, until I naturally forgot about it. Then at the age of eight or so, we were dressing for Church on a Sunday morning. Suddenly I remembered this infantile motion that once so secretly united us, and wanted to put my finger into the hidden store of food between her breasts. She reacted with fear, which I could not understand and she roughly rejected me.

Deep down in our souls, my mother and I knew in that moment that I would remember this as long as I was alive, but we would never talk about it. The glass wall of shame filtered the sensual beauty of our bodies and the world. We could see each other but were no longer allowed to touch neither with hands nor with words.

My parents hid their passionate feelings for each other, too, as if it was sin, and thus they made us feel uncomfortable with ourselves and our sexuality. Instead of buying into this game, we both started going out with boys very early. We also were secretive about our relationships and never talked about them to our parents. It was simply impossible to admit that we had an interest in the opposite sex. Our parents' double standards concerning sexuality made our family life stiff and joyless. Although we loved our parents and each other dearly, we were longing to grow up and get away from them. They did not allow frivolities or dirty jokes in the house either.

When I entered, the stark purity grabbed my throat with cold fingers. All of a sudden I was turned into the old sensible Saoirse, and I felt immediately depressed.

My mother looked at the motorbike with great concern.

'Lovely to see you, pet. We've been looking forward to you coming home.'

'Mum, this is my friend. His name is Gerry Tanner. Isn't it awful?'

'Nobody chooses their own name.'

She was smiling at Gerry uncertainly. Gerry gave her a big, good-boyish smile:

'Good evening, Mrs. Connell. Please call me Gerry. It is what my mum calls me, too.'

My mother was still reluctant; the motorbike obviously confused her:

'That's kind, come in, please.'

Going into the living room, I knew exactly how Gerry was feeling. He was irritated, and the skin tightened on his face. He resisted the urge to run away, but when he realized that it was not possible anyway, he became angry and hid his anger behind a defensive contempt. My blood froze at the thought what the next hours would bring to light.

As we entered the living room, I was no longer able to recognize the safe nest of my childhood. The walls felt narrow and overwhelming, only the statue of Mary was looking at me with the same mellow eyes from her pedestal in the left-hand corner, opposite the television. Her glimpse, full of compassion, gave me the strength to believe in my love for all these hostile parties, who were brought together to take part in and to reluctantly influence that crucial moment of my life.

My fifteen-year-old sister, Laura, jumped into my arms, while she was staring at Gerry with great curiosity. My father stood up from the table and embraced me, and then he turned to Gerry who was not smiling. He looked rather bored and annoyed. They shook hands.

My mother hurried there to give my father the false information, stating that Gerry was from Belfast. She just pushed the button that triggered the following chain reaction of mistakes and mischief, which eventually would lead to my destruction.

I corrected her mistake:

'No, I know him from Lurgan. He is a musician.'

My father did not think highly of artists, I knew. I could have been diplomatic and massage the truth by saying that he studied the science of music, but this solution seemed too ridiculous. I did not feel like putting on any mask, and I had to show Gerry that I loved and respected him.

My mother was trying to involve Gerry in a conversation, as he had not said a word yet.

'Oh, really, Saoirse has played the organ since she was a small child. She used to play here in our church. Before she went to Belfast she even played for mass. She is very talented.'

Gerry looked at me amazed. His look was full of playful recognition and it energized me. I had to hide my feelings, however, as my father was examining my every move.

'Oh, Mum, I wouldn't call that music.'

Then Laura joined the choir:

'Only Saoirse's modesty can surpass her talent. Isn't it true, Dad?'

He had to reply, had to loosen his stiffness a little; he had to give in to the innocent Laura's pleas. He did not know that Laura was playing a part in this theatre just as my mother and me.

'Our daughter is very intelligent, it's true.'

Gerry still did not speak and I felt that everything was lost.

He had lunch with us. Laura and I tried to lighten the atmosphere by joking about teachers and city life, but Dad and Gerry hardly talked to each other.

It was getting dark when he was about to leave and I said good-bye to him in front of the house. The whole family was watching us from behind the curtains when we were kissing, but I did not care. I was not sure when I would ever see him again. I suddenly felt that the end of the world was round the corner. I asked him anxiously:

'Will you write to me?'

'Can anybody else read your e-mails?'

'No, I'll make that sure.'

'Then I will write to you my dirty e-mails.'

He said it like the wicked wolf to the goat in a fairy tale and we burst out laughing. He suddenly stopped and became serious: 'How will you get away from here?'

'Don't worry about it. I definitely will get away. Leave that to me. Promise to write to me.'

'I cross my heart and hope to die. Leo's cottage will be free for the whole of August. In Bangor. Will you come there?'

'Before August I should be able to come to Lurgan, too. I'd like to be with you always.'

He laughed at this with delight, and suddenly the whole world changed. We escaped from the airless serenity of my parental house. He bowed towards the family behind the curtains knowing that they were our invisible audience:

'May I introduce Roo, the honored friend of Winnie the Pooh, your new English teacher?'

We laughed and he left, blowing kisses at me. I followed his diminishing silhouette with my eyes till it disappeared at the end of the street. The red light of the motorbike swam on the tears on my iris. I sat down on the steps of the front door. This was my favorite place at home, where I could think undisturbed. More and more stars appeared in the sky and I could count eight of them, and made a wish. I wished to be able to go to Bangor without problems and that my parents would understand my needs.

I felt lost. I knew that my father had branded our relationship, even before Gerry's appearance. Gerry sensed his resistance and did not want to please him either, because of being too proud or rebellious, I was not sure. I knew that it would be very difficult to get away from home in the summer. I always hated dishonesty, and now my existence was dependent on it. I could only be happy with lying.

Out in the Heat

During the summer holidays Saoirse stayed at home in Newry, under the watchful eyes of her parents, her father especially tried to keep her away from Gerry, who by then had become his arch enemy. She spent suspiciously long hours at the computer, reading and writing e-mails. The parents did not know and therefore could not control their communication, Saoirse pretended to be studying or researching. The intensity of these love messages took her away into a virtual world. On the planes of the mind they were free and together. Gerry's sudden love for the computer was met with the same perplexity at his mother's house in Lurgan.

Gerry felt that he needed to fight for CC to get her away from home during the summer, and explained his dissonant feelings in a long letter to her:

> *Darling CC,*
> *I have to be honest with you; I was maddened by your oldies. They are modest, rigid do-goodies. I do not know which is worse, to be modest or to be rigid, but the two qualities coupled together had a suffocating effect on me and something changed you, too. I understand if you did not notice, for you grew up in that atmosphere,*

but their show of Goodness and Morale made me senseless and nauseous from the first second on. I did know how to defend myself.

I hated the outskirts of Newry if such a thing exists, for the whole Newry seemed to be suburbia to me. The pastel wallpaper in the hall must be your mother's favorite and it reminded me of my Auntie Maeve's. It looked the same before me and my bro started our spitting championships. The family pictures did not impress me except for little Saoirse on her first day of school in crisp uniform, smiling bravely into the camera. Proud Mr. Connell with his wife and two daughters gazed at me from another picture and I began to feel annoyed. The whole house smelled of myrrh and it felt as if I was not allowed to look at anywhere else but either at the icons of Mr. Connell's perfect family or at the floor. They called you 'Saoirse,' and this transformed my girl into their slave. (Even though the name means freedom. I still can't understand why they gave you this name, if they have no idea what it means.) You became very stiff and your smile lost the naughty glamour that I love so much.

When your mother greeted us at the door I could see on her face that she was not sure whether her husband would allow her to like me, so it was best to remain on neutral grounds with me. Therefore she led us into the dining room where I could be scrutinized and tried by your father. He shook my hand in a terribly masculine manner and I, if my memory does not lie, must have reacted too slowly, because he hated me from that moment. He was not the first father in my life who had no other emotion than contempt for me. His hatred did not bother me very much, but it clearly hurt you, I could see.

Do not worry, honey. Concentrate with all your powers on getting away from there. I know you will succeed. I will be waiting for you in Belfast or in Bangor. I will be training my body to be strong for you and to make you happy, to compensate you for all that suffering in that house of pink horrors.
I love you and miss you, please come soon.
Gerry

When Saoirse read the letter she cried, she was so shaken by his feelings and the fact that she detected them during that fateful visit, she felt them all. It was a written confirmation of how deeply connected they were.

The summer was overshadowed by nothing but secret appointments. In August Gerry went to Bangor, to Leo's parents' cottage. Leo, faithfully following his Gandhian philanthropy, always organized big parties there, and his parents, being high-class logical thinkers, gave their blessing to them. They accepted the all-pervading hormonal changes in their son and his friends, knowing that they could not be worked against. Leo's father, who was an advocator and joyous practitioner of the sexual revolution in the seventies, was relieved by the sheer hope that his son, finally, would lose his virginity. In their family the generation conflict presented itself in a highly absurd way. Leo rebelled against his father by turning to metaphysics instead of science, and retaining his virginity or at least showing reluctance to decide which sexual group he belonged to, which was even worse in the eyes of a heterosexual scientist. Whenever they had time or opportunity to talk, Leo's father gently brought up the possibility of an informal chat with his good friend, a psychiatrist, by the way, but luckily he was too occupied with his job and never really got to arranging an appointment. The summer seemed to be therefore, the last chance for Leo to sort out the matter for himself, before his father got to the bottom of it, by employing an expert who would happily dissect his son's mind. Leo did not know which prospect was more terrifying, being deflowered by an experienced female or being screwed up by a psychiatrist. He told Gerry about his dilemma, but regretted it when he realized that Gerry transformed the issue into his own crusade.

Leo, Lord and Gerry spent their days with playing music and they had a good time. Gerry spent days with coaching Leo in the art of courtship, trying to pick up a certain girl on the beach, but it never happened. Gerry was getting really cross with him, especially when Leo told him to give up. Angry over his friend's lameness, Gerry finally pushed himself to ask Leo about that mysterious sheet of paper he had found in his bedroom in the spring when he had used Leo's room as a love-nest.

'You are not interested in your success at all, Leo.'

'No, I want something special and that might take time to get.'

'That's all right. But would you tell me then how come that you know exactly what passion is about?'

'I know it instinctively.'

'You know, Leo. I did see some writings in your room when I tidied up. That was so explicit that I am sure you are dreaming about someone.'

'I must be a good dreamer,' Leo answered lazily. 'But joking apart, I do automatic writing.'

'What's that?'

'You take a pencil to a piece of paper and a force beyond you starts to write.'

'A ghost?'

'Nobody knows exactly. Ghosts, past lives, your own alter-egos. The Creator in you. You should try it, too.'

Leo, bright as he was, managed to talk himself out of the catch, Gerry could not do anything else, but believe him. He knew that Leo would not lie to him, or at least not if it was important. Gerry wanted to believe in someone's honest friendship and his choice fell on Leo a very long time before. So he started to do automatic writing and amazing things started to happen to him. His creativity improved immensely and he composed wonderful new lyrics for Leo's music. Something was awakening the passion in him, too, and he could only thank Leo for the experience. He compared his newly found passion to Leo's and he could see what the difference between the two was. He thought that his was real, for he could not control it like Leo, who just played at it. Gerry's passion took oversized measures and made him do things he would have never ever done, or at least he thought so.

To Gerry's joy, Saoirse appeared in the cottage on a Friday afternoon. He had given up hope already; therefore he was amazed and delighted at the same time. She was taking along Aoife, a friend of hers from Newry. They could have had more than forty-eight hours entirely to themselves, but Gerry, the passionate animal, instead of enjoying the time with Saorise; started to flirt with her friend. Not to say that Aoife was such a good 'ride' or that she had had a charismatic personality. No, he simply let himself go.

They went to the beach for a naked swim on Saturday night. Leo, perhaps just in order to please Gerry, had been trying his luck with Aoife since the girls had arrived in the evening and he seemed to be getting somewhere, but he gave up on her too early. Gerry had seen this happen with other girls many times before and it annoyed him. He could now easily see what Leo's real problem was. He definitely lacked self-confidence. When the unlucky chap's steam started to run out he drunk more wine in order to gain courage, but he overdid it at the end.

They stumbled down the graveled path to the beach in the moonlight, the stones crunching under their feet. Leo and Aoife walked in the middle, visibly inebriated, bumping into each other, while Saoirse and Gerry on their outer sides, playing the sober protectors. They all took off their clothes on the shore, except for Leo.

'I can't go into this cold water, no way,' he mumbled.

'It wouldn't harm you,' Gerry and CC said in unison. Then they giggled. Saorise ran into the water screaming and laughing, like a siren.

Leo lay down on their clothes on the beach, delving in profound melancholy and staring into nothingness. Aoife, now uselessly naked, seemed to have lost her patience. She gave up waiting for Leo's appearance on stage. Taking the initiative, she utterly strained herself to give the boys the impression that her slink body levitating into the water was a natural phenomenon. She hoped to wake the sleeping lion in Leo, or as a matter of fact in anybody, if there was one. When the water reached up her thighs, she started to turn around; swinging her arms and breasts in the moonshine, but Leo showed no reaction.

Gerry was pre-empting what would happen and turned to Leo with anger.

'What does the woman do? She turns to someone else. This is part of their genetic make-up, too. They need to be conquered or to believe that they have conquered.'

Leo did not reply.

'I am that someone else at hand. And I will show you,' Aoife screamed out. On her round bottom, the moon was laughing delightfully in the water drops. Gerry waded to her like a real hero. His thing was dangling like a sword.

'A shell!'

While she was falling, all the hungry lions lying around could have had a glimpse between her darkly exciting thighs, if they had cared.

Gerry pulled Aoife to the shore. She overdid her drunkenness and leaned with all her weight on him. Gerry examined the sole of her foot. He talked for Leo:

'We'll make it better. First, you have to clean the cut. There must be some bandaging stuff in the house.'

He passed the catchword to Leo who only snarled incomprehensibly as a sign of his agreement, and then returned to observe his majestic silence.

Saoirse was swimming away now.

'The water is fantastic, come in, Gerry!'

'I'm coming!' Gerry grinned at Aoife who understood the joke.

Meanwhile, keeping Aoife's foot in one hand, he showed off his skills and pulled a towel on her back with his other hand. When he finished his job Saoirse was already on the shore. She called for him using a tone of voice that he did not like at all.

'Come, Gerry, I want to talk to you.'

Gerry was chuckling with laughter, for Aoife was ticklish. Her foot was frisking about in his palms and he kept grabbing for it as though it were a slippery fish.

'OK. I'm coming,' he said, but when he looked up Saoirse was gone.

In his anger about her leaving him on the spot, he became even nicer to Aoife. The atmosphere changed suddenly and everybody sobered up. They set out for the house. On the way, seeing that Leo didn't want her, Gerry gave Aoife his undivided attention.

Things got even worse when CC was not in the house. She had just left a note thanking Leo for his hospitality, and giving a lame excuse that she did not feel well and wanted to go home. She also wrote that she went to the station to catch a train, which could have meant an invitation for Gerry to follow her and make it up with her. Everybody expected Gerry to do so, but he became furious and got further involved with Aoife, so much that they really began a kind of an affair. If it was to be, let it be. CC wanted it.

Gerry could put up with Aoife for the next day only, but when he went back to Belfast to see his gang, all of his friends knew that CC had finished with him.

Games and Pastimes

September passed leaving Gerry empty. Starting back at school, indifferent every day, brooding over the memories of the summer. He started to date Judy, lazily thinking she would cheer him up. He nurtured these high hopes because it all began in a very strange way and there was a kind of magic or precognition in the air again.

They were standing in front of the school one morning. Gerry was blowing the smoke into the fog of the early October sunshine. Gerry was bored and looked around for some amusement. His eyes caught sight of Judy.

She had long brown hair, her tan was still dark from the summer heat and she had lavish long fingernails. She soon sensed that Gerry was watching her and she swiped down the crowd that was blocking the view between them with her big brown, cow-like eyes. She sent investigating glimpses back at him over the dead bodies, as Gerry saw it.

Then Lord arrived and distracted his attention for a while:

'I have a commission for you.'

'A ten quid or five packs of cigarettes.'

'You have to write a love poem for Yoyosh.'

'It'll be fifteen quid for him, he is too stupid.'

'Stop fooling about, he won't pay as much as that.'

He was not in the mood to put up with Lord's negativity in an early morning before school; thus he carried on without explanation.

'Exactly that's why, he will.'

Seeing this resistance, Lord started hitting him under the belt in his usual good-willing manner:

'I think, you write every poem for CC, don't you?'

'Where did you get this idea?'

'Last time you wrote a poem for Zooloo, remember? Well, I kept it for a day or so to read it a couple of times.'

'Why do you want to analyze me?'

'You were really crazy in Bangor. In my opinion you still have a chance to fix everything up with CC.'

'I don't think so. I'm quite sure that she doesn't love me anymore. And now leave me alone.'

They dropped their cigarettes and entered the building. Three girls, among them Judy, followed them. The girls were giggling. Gerry detested Lord for having touched a painful spot in him. In order to show Lord how little interested he was in CC, he turned back to the girls. He stepped to Judy and said something that he did not really know anything about, but he was a master of improvisation:

'You should try it. It will be OK.'

Judy had obviously expected something else as she asked him perplexed:

'What?'

Gerry wanted to turn her upside down and shake out her cow eyes and he suggested to her with a more than impudent grin:

'Making love with him.'

Her look made him believe that she would forget to shut her mouth for the next day or so. He did not know that she had been complaining about her father just five minutes before.

He made an impression, with sheer bravura, and he could be sure that she would go out with her.

Gerry soon started to play his own mind games with her that he enjoyed a lot. She was a girl that could make one think for a while, and she suffered a lot because of her father who regarded her as his property.

It was true that Gerry had never met a father who would not have liked to put his daughter into a showcase. In this event, however, there was an interesting point. Judy was in love with her heartless tyrant. Gerry found this out as soon as during their first date, sitting at the shore of the Lagan River:

'He hates every guy around me. He did try to persuade me not to go out with any of the boys I wanted to. I didn't take his advice, but it often turned out that he was right.'

'Therefore, he's always right?'

'Yes. I realized that he can't be compared to anybody else. He is incredibly intelligent.'

'I don't agree, having heard what you've had to say about him.'

'He trained as a lawyer, but now he is in advertising.'

'My father used to be a spy in Cairo.'

'Was he? What is he now?'

'Dead.'

'Oh, I'm sorry.'

'Don't be. He was a hero. Anyway, your father can't be very intelligent if he keeps you confined like this.'

'He's worried about me. He has no idea that he could be hurting me with it.'

'Oh, the poor devil. But you're in love with him, aren't you?'

'Generally, all little girls are in love with their fathers, but it's another kind of love. A sort of respect or something like that.'

'Or idolizing. I've already told you what to do.'

'What did you tell me? I don't remember.'

'You know, I've already told you to make love with him, if you adore him so much. It's just a natural conclusion.'

'You're crazy, this is disgusting!' Judy was screaming as if she had seen a rat.

Yes, Gerry was crazy, but this was exactly the thing girls adored about him. The next minute, instead of slapping his face, she was kissing him.

The game was over. Gerry won again. Bored to death, he looked over to the other shore, where the waves were splashing an empty rowboat, driving it deeper into the mud. There was a heap of cement sacks, but nobody waving at him. He closed his eyes, trying to enjoy that stolen kiss, but to his utmost anger and annoyance it was impossible.

After having revealed Judy's complex he kept teasing her at each of their encounters, from the beginning till the end. Arriving, he often greeted her with the question:

'Have you made love already?' or:

'Have you had sex, my daughter?'

He enjoyed her confusion, which was nothing else than powerless protest against the instincts. He had good reason to assume that he had managed to smuggle Judy's father into her erotic dreams. The thought gave him devilish satisfaction, but even this pervert success could not divert his attention from the yawning emptiness inside him and from the fact that he was longing for CC. Had he grown up suddenly? All his being wanted CC. He wanted to sink into her sensuality, and forget his games, get lost in her.

Was it a fortunate accident or was it inevitable that he missed the train to Belfast one day and she was standing in front of him on the platform? The train was on its way from Newry to Belfast and if he had not missed it, he would have missed her. It was peculiar enough that she had just written some lines to him on the train. When Gerry saw her he knew everything. 'I love you' was the message written on her face, there was no need for any note. She pressed the sheet into his hand and quickly turned to go, but Gerry stopped her, hugging her and lifting her up as if wanting to melt her into himself. There was no way he would have let her go.

Forces

That autumn Sister O'Hara warned Saoirse that she would be suspended if she was not prepared to keep to the regulations. They shortened the leash, which meant that she was only allowed to go out in the evening once a week. It all had to be thoroughly organized, whenever she asked for permission she was expected to show some kind of evidence of her planned whereabouts, a theatre or cinema ticket.

Saoirse suffered terribly in the convent, where even culture was a measure of discipline. She could not be with Gerry as often as she wished, while she was very conscious of her duty to study for her exams. To make this pulling apart even harder to bear, Sister O'Hara found strange delight in delivering lectures to her and her friends about personal responsibility.

At the beginning of November Saoirse wanted to go with Gerry to a concert of the Mozart Requiem that was going to be held in a Presbyterian church. She didn't get permission. Sister O'Hara argued that the concert clashed with a rehearsal for the school's prize giving ceremony, where Saoirse was going to recite a poem. She did not dare to risk missing the rehearsal against Sister O'Hara's will, but the unfair ban drove her into despair. She knew that she was the victim of a senseless sectarian policy. Sister O'Hara managed to deprive her of regaining inner calm with Mozart in a church and only because the concert was to be held in a Protestant parish. As Gerry had pointed out to her it was a one-time opportunity, for he knew the church in question with its extraordinary acoustic.

Gerry witnessed her breaking down, with regret admitting that Mozart's music could have worked miracles, as it always did for him, too. It was too late, CC missed her chance.

Nobody could have stopped him from going anywhere he wanted to go, but he knew well where to push and where to pull. He was careful enough to play his cards right at his mixed school. In this case he was willing to compromise. His priority was the music and his was the best of the few integrated colleges with a musical faculty in the county. Integrated meant that pupils of all creeds and abilities were admitted. This created a strange mixture of people and there were oddballs like himself with whom he could have fun with. They knew that their parents wanted peace in Northern Ireland and the fact that they sent them into a mixed secondary school was their statement. However, peace-loving parents did not guarantee peaceful children, and there were gangs and hostilities among the pupils, just like anywhere else in their society. Nevertheless, their parents' intent mattered a lot and it was a privilege to be a member of that community. The pupils at the musical faculty built a kind of elite in the school and for Gerry this special status was extremely important, and that his talent was acknowledged and counted for.

He knew that some teachers tended to deny him this pleasure of personal success, but they would have taken away any pleasure from him if they could. He subscribed this antagonism to simple male competition. Some of the most hated teachers like 'Mr. Queer' picked him out sometimes, but what could he have done? He paid the price and danced to his queer music.

Once he went to the loo for a smoke, and found most of the boys from the neighboring class there. One could cut the smoke with a knife. Fujiyama, the most popular one from that class, was there, too, and Gerry knew when he saw him that they would have some fun very soon. The boy was a heavily built monster as Gerry saw him, and belonged to the species of men that he simply called big dicks—not as if they really possessed big instruments, no, they just imagined that they did. Gerry used to play pranks on Fuji, whenever he could, exploiting the huge difference between their IQs.

Fujiyama was boasting with his most probably only talent, 'turn the fag and fume.' Only with the skills of his slimy dripping lips he managed to turn the burning fag into his mouth. When the cigarette was inside, he blew the smoke through his nose and ears, and he became terribly red and ridiculous. The others always watched this disgusting show with great amazement, including Leo and Lord, resulting in giving him the nickname of a fuming volcano. When Gerry arrived, Fujiyama started mocking him:

'The Prince from Cairo has arrived.'

'What's up, Fujiyama?' Gerry asked him, pointing at his fag.

'Damn you!' Fuji replied kindly.

Gerry went into a cubicle. Suddenly a flash of light went up in his mind and he shouted to the guys hanging around outside:

'Oh, it reminds me. Queer's loitering around the door.'

Everybody put out his cigarette, like madmen. Gerry was laughing inside the loo, when to his greatest surprise he could actually hear the door opening and Queer entering.

Gerry was gob-smacked by his precognition. He was often able to guess or feel what people would reply in the next minute in the course of a discussion, but this was the first time that he could actually foretell someone's action. In this second, hearing Queer's voice from outside, a range of past events ran through his head, which he had held for luck or coincidence. They all began to gain a certain meaning. He was very close to believing that he had supernatural power, but he did not have time to indulge himself in these thoughts. He had to face the narrow and limited world of his Geography teacher first. Queer's voice rolled like thunder through the sudden silence:

'What is this mass-urination here?'

Gerry could not help, but burst out laughing. Hearing his laughter from behind the closed door, Queer came to the cubicle and called him:

'Come out at once!'

When he opened the door Gerry could see Fujiyama's face as he was almost suffocating from the smoke: the cigarette was still burning in his mouth! Gerry was laughing like a horse. Queer turned to Fuji, with his lop-sided lips trying to imply that he had a sense of humor after all:

'If you're sick, go and vomit.'

At this point everybody started choking. Fuji turned into the cubicle with relief. He was retching and coughing at the same time. Queer had to keep his face and shake off the heavy weight of his anger thus he pointed at Gerry:

'And what about you, young man. Why are you laughing?'

'Excuse me, sir,' Gerry said, swallowing his pride. 'Something reminded me of the Fuji Mountain.'

This started a wave of suffocating giggle in the background and Gerry felt rewarded for his bravery.

'Yes, son, and what would be so funny about that? That it all went up in smoke?'

At this point nothing could stop the tide of laughter in the background. The teacher turned to the others:

'I'll remember your faces! As soon as you have finished, get out of here!'

Gerry never believed that Sister O'Hara would have ever get CC expelled, although she often threatened to do so. After all, no matter how cruel they were, all the wardens were aware of their responsibility for the girls. It was like a vicious circle: the more they felt responsible the meaner they became, which drove the girls into fiercer rebellion.

They kept the girls well and truly locked up, dead on. This had a reverse effect on everybody. For Gerry it was a challenge; the more he wanted to be with CC, and she even managed to sneak out for a few weekends. In the hostel she said that she would go home. Gerry forged her mother's signature on the leaving note. For the family she invented some excursions or a visit to a girlfriend's remote village, preferably somewhere in the north, where there was no mobile phone coverage.

Besides all of this anxiety Saoirse was worried that she might get pregnant. She was too frightened to consult her GP, who was great friends with her parents.

At the beginning they were sensible enough, but after a while, beyond reason, they stopped using contraception. It could not be explained with the growing trust they had for each other, on the contrary, after Gerry's adventure with Aoifa there was a certain tension between them. Saoirse was often distrustful, though Gerry tried his best to restore her faith in himself as far as he was able to.

They knew very well that it was dangerous to make love. Gerry believed that Saoirse wanted to lift all boundaries between them, so that they could be deeply connected again and this was her way of healing the rift. They both knew that it was possible; for once they had achieved it with the synchronicity game, when they were open for each other without limits, free and bound at the same time, but Gerry's cheating on her tore those fine threads apart.

While Gerry felt guilty towards Saoirse, he could easily excuse his own fooling around with other girls. Girls adored him always, he just gave in to them, and he made everyone believe that this was his birthright for freedom. On the other hand, it was really only fooling. They did not mean much to him, they were simply playmates and he never made love with anybody else after the mischief with Aoifa. There were flirts and brief kisses, but nothing more. He was only silly and endlessly tactless for mentioning them to her in ambiguous ways so that she could fantasize about them. Like a peacock opening its feathery tail, boasting to attract interest. He was selfish, but he told himself that he was actually honest. This was selfish, too, but he did not want to lie to her about anything.

That autumn they wrote letters to each other. It seemed old-fashioned when they could have sent text massages or e-mails, but it was a way for him to sneak into her life his thoughts and feelings physically, his need to be with her was extreme. Gerry begged for money from the girls at school for stamps and wrote love poems for his insane schoolmates in return for money or cigarettes. If they were so silly to pay. It was easy for him: he was a fountain of words, for he wrote all those love poems for CC.

Under his fears, bravado and confusions, he was sure that she would understand him. He had no need for excuses. For Gerry it was vital that she had the capacity to grow into a friend, even though she knew that Gerry could not help but pick up some girls from time to time. For Gerry there was nothing more important than to be allowed to be honest, regardless of hurting. Her answer was love.

The Virgin

Gerry had little understanding for Saoirse when she was willing to accept the boundary her parents set between her and him. He knew that her studies were important to her and she wanted to get into university, but he expected more loyalty from her. He thought that he earned it with his honesty, not knowing that creases could not be ironed so easily in a woman's heart.

When they saw each other again on the twenty-eighth of December, he asked her how long was she willing to be the slave of her family.

'I can't understand, you were one of the top bunkers at the hostel. How is it possible that you can't explain to your parents that you'd be safe and that you have a right to stay with me?'

'Gerry, this is my world. You are incapable of seeing, not to mention feeling it, because you've never been shown boundaries, you always did what you wanted. They think I'm a helpless virgin. If they allow me to stay out then it won't take long and they'll have to allow my little sister, too. After all they never know me safe on your side, no; you stand for the biggest danger, in fact. My father doesn't like artists; he said you'd never earn money. They want to see the future husband in you and you are even younger than me.'

113

She spoke out the last words with a funny gesture, pulling her nose up. The whole assumption seemed utterly ridiculous and Gerry could not do any better, but to join her giggle.

'Me husband? I've never heard such absurdity.'

Of course, Gerry got what he wanted. It could not be otherwise. They went to Orla's party that night. With Orla's help they created a plot to convince Saoirse's parents that she had to stay in Lurgan for the night. Gerry took her to his place.

It was a night full of mystery. Snow fell and they walked home on foot in the cold with the Orion above them. The sky had an orange shimmer at the edges of the horizon, where the streetlights met the open space. Gerry looked up at the red giant that had made him gape from his early childhood on.

'Do you see that trapezoidal constellation there? That is the Orion.'

'Yes, I know. When I was a little girl and I was sad, I sat down on the steps at our front door and watched the stars. Later I even learned the names of some of the stars by heart. Do you know them?'

Gerry just shook his head.

'Well, the red one on the left is Betelgeuse, facing it Bellatrix. They are like sisters. I never felt alone when there was a starry night. I used to think that somewhere, out there a little girl was doing the same what I did. She was standing on her planet, staring out into the universe. For her the Earth was just a blue star, and we looked at each other.'

'Yes, this sounds like a mirror. But the mirror cannot let you in. It can only reflect what you do.'

'That's right. This idea does not comfort me any longer. I've found a better mirror who can let me in, in whom I recognized myself and who made me possible to love myself. Do you know who that is?'

Of course, he knew, but she did not expect an answer. Her cheeks were red from the icy air. The snow's white reflected in her eyes like a remote star and Gerry saw on that star a little boy who has been abandoned by his father not long ago and sat down on the steps outside their front door, to be comforted by the stars. He stared into his eyes and whispered between his teeth:

'Don't say anything but give me your tongue, hold my bottom, tear me to pieces.'

When he kissed her she closed her eyes. He embraced her, wanting to press her soul into his.

They slept together in Gerry's bed. They were not careful they did not bother about anything, as if it had been their last opportunity to be together, as if each minute were a gift.

Saoirse set out early in the morning to reach her train. She was strained and guilt-ridden. Gerry asked her to think it over and slip away somehow on New Year's Eve. Eventually they agreed that they would only see each other in the New Year.

On New Year's Eve Gerry was totally drunk. He picked up a stray girl at Billy Gate's club. It did not mean much to him; they kissed and danced all night that was all. For the girl he was a one-night stand, too, he would never see her again. But Saoirse was deeply hurt. She felt that it was not her fault that she could not be with Gerry and that he had abandoned her.

The next time after Gerry had told her of this occurrence he waited for her in front of the school on January sixth. He was walking up and down there in order not to miss her leaving. She was sad and vacant looking. Gerry accompanied her to the bus and was trying to get her into a conversation.

'Well, how did you spend the weekend?'

'Not as well as you spent your New Year's Eve. You know, Gerry, I was waiting for you all that night. You could have abducted me.'

Gerry had no answer to this reproach. The truth was that the hunter passion had overcome him again, but he could impossibly admit that. He said in his most disinterested manner what fifty-year-old power-freaks would say to their wives:

'Things took a different turn.'

He knew that he was making a mistake for he was lying, but he was fed up with the sadness he had been causing. As if answering his thought she said:

'Sorry, it's too late.'

'What do you mean?'

'I mean that I'm tired, and I have had enough. I'm sick of the way you treat me.'

Indeed, she looked very tired.

'Does this mean that it's all over?' Gerry asked her incredibly.

'You are too childish. I need someone who understands me who lets me feel that he loves me.'

'Love and sex are two different matters.'

'Not with me.'

They arrived at the bus stop. Gerry kissed her forehead without saying a word and left her there. She did not look into his eyes and his heart almost broke. After six steps he turned back to check whether she had her eyes on him. Just in case, he had already decided that he would control the situation with a grin, as he always did. Of course, she was watching! She did not turn away her eyes when they met his, but facing her grave features he suddenly became lamed, he could not grin at all.

Gerry asked Leo to approach her in order to find out whether she still loved him. It was characteristic of their relationship that he was not sure, though if there was anyone who knew women well, then it was him. But she loved him. He borrowed his old letters from her on the pretext of wanting to write a short story. He read them and wrote new ones for her every day.

It took all his efforts to keep the fire of love alive in her. It seemed as if he was desperately blowing and blowing the glowing embers, but he did not give it up. First he could entice her for a theatre play. Later she became eighteen thus she was allowed to go out more often. During this time they talked more. Gerry got to know her better than ever before and he realized that he wanted only this girl. Although she was a bit formal with him, he was certain that one day he would win her over, she would believe him again. He had no doubts that she was steady in her love like a rock, and he knew that this time he would change. Something snapped in him and he wanted to be good, loving, trustworthy and reliable. He wanted to be her man.

Death Again

Some time later, at the beginning of March Saoirse said something that blew Gerry's world apart.

'I like going out with you, Gerry; I think you are a good friend. I think, I owe you this confession about my trouble,' she sighed. 'I'm pregnant.'

In his surprise Gerry barely could say anything. He did not intend to hurt her, but he asked her a question that he should have never had:

'Who's it from?'

She pulled the left edge of her mouth painfully to the side: 'You.'

A long silence followed that seemed to create an abyss between them, yet Gerry could not utter a word.

'I've been thinking about it a lot and decided not to keep it. I'm going to Liverpool end of next week.'

Gerry took a deep breath. He knew that this was the moment to fight. The desert rose in him and a little boy was begging for his life.

'You mustn't abort my child. Think it over, I love you. I'll marry you or whatever you want. The two of us and a child, wouldn't that be wonderful?'

When he did not see any effect of his words on her face he nearly burst out crying:

'That's like killing me in yourself, don't you understand? I know that you love me and you will always love me. Why do you want to kill me?'

In reply she gave him all those cold and sensible reasons:

'You cannot think realistically. You are sixteen and I am just eighteen. And I cannot trust you anymore. I can only trust myself. I want to carry on with my studies.'

'You can't abort my child. If you do that, then everything will be over between us.'

'Everything was already over on New Year's Eve,' she replied bitterly, pressing the words out of her mouth.

Then she turned her back to him and hurried away on her dreadful mission, leaving him behind in the middle of the empty street that now seemed like a boiling ocean of sand.

Gerry did not dare to admit to anybody, not even to himself what he felt. Abandoned again, terribly incomplete, as if an important part of him had left him, as if he had lost a leg or even his penis had been amputated. He had to release all that anger he felt. Yes, she had only contempt for him, when she decided about the fate of their baby without asking him, when she just simply made up her mind to get rid of it and to get rid of him at the same time. She displayed the whole universe's disgust at him. She played the same terrible God that took his father from him such a long time before, she, the woman he loved.

The following week was a nightmare. Gerry was chasing CC everywhere. He did apply all his powers. He tried to talk to her in his dreams, always pleading, fighting to stop her. He did not know how she was planning to go to Liverpool. He tried to phone Laura, CC's sister, but she was just as cold and resolute as CC herself. On Friday he spent hours at the Belfast train station, waiting for trains from Newry, then at the harbor, watching the ferries, until he got the idea of checking the passenger lists of the airplanes. It was his tragedy that she was already on the way to Liverpool when he found her name on one of the lists. The nice woman at the information counter gave him the time of CC's flight back on Sunday, not knowing how fatally late that time would be for him. Nevertheless, he went to the airport just in order to tread into her for the very last time.

When she appeared in the arrival gate, her face was greenish white and he could see that she was desperate. She looked at him scared.

'How was it?' Gerry asked with his most cynical grin on the face.

'It was terrible and if you've only come to hurt me, then you'd better go.'

'I'll go, don't worry. I just wanted to look into the eyes of the murderer for the last time. This image will keep me going my way.'

Her eyes became round with pain and slowly brimmed over with tears.

'Farewell,' Gerry said, turning his back at her.

He did not hear about her for months. He stayed in touch with her cousin Orla, or rather; she stayed in touch with Gerry. She phoned him from time to time and gossiped about CC. Gerry knew that she was preparing for the A-levels, and she did them very well. Then she got a place at Queen's University just as she had wished. Gerry had all reasons to think that she was doing well, being happy, but he did not want to know. He found these phone calls rather boring and one day he told Orla to leave him alone with her unsolicited news service, for CC was dead. He had nothing to do with her anymore.

At school Lord tried to doctor his inner world. Gerry was truly surrounded by good will, which he could hardly ever stand.

One day Lord was trying to coax Gerry into some statement about CC. Gerry could not decide whether Lord was cross that she did not favor him after Gerry or he was just trying to poke the dagger deeper into his heart.

'Leo is going out with CC,' he said with a certain curiosity in his voice.

'It will do them good. Do you want me to console you?'

'No. I just need a poem from you for my personal use.'

Gerry was fed up with his one-time agent. Lord was always trying to exploit his talents:

'For a new bird?'

'Yes. For Andy, from 10 LK.'

'Give her the poem I wrote for Cathy last year. I won't write any more for you. What am I? A love machine? In any event I hate women now.'

'And when did you ever love them? You little sex pistol.'

Even he turned against Gerry.

Then all of a sudden, Gerry got a letter from CC herself, but he sent it back without opening it. Liam reported to him that she had been coming to the family house frequently, waiting for Gerry deep into the night, and having long chats with Ma. Gerry felt lucky for having managed to keep clear of her. By that time Seamus spent most of the week at their home with Ma and Liam and Gerry often stayed with friends in the city when he was not in the mood to face his jolly jokes.

Whenever he chose to go home, he did it late at night and he often scared his mother with his silent arrivals, as if he had been a stranger or a criminal. He really felt that he did not belong anywhere. He could only explain his rudeness with the overwhelming hate for the world, but especially for women:

'Hello. What's up? Aren't you glad to see me?' he asked his mother on coming home at half eleven one night.

'Haven't you met Saoirse, she's just left?'

'No. Thank God.'

'She is such a nice girl, Gerry. I think, she is in love with you.'

'Is she? I wish she would leave me alone.' His mother gave up on the subject, but dutifully started to foster him:

'Where did you sleep this week? At least you should have the decency to phone me, when you decide to stay out.'

He said sorry, though he did not mean it, and hugged her. She melted in his arms. Then she passed on to him a note that CC had left. Reluctantly, and because it was an open letter he started to read:

Dear Gerry,
There is so much I have to tell you. I feel so sorry for all that happened between us. Please give me a chance to explain it. Please do not refuse me anymore. I need to talk to you.
Love
CC

These words had no effect on him; he tore up the piece of paper and went to sleep. He entered the darkness of the night that seemed to inhabit his heart now. When dreams came he could be sure they would be better than his reality. The desert was calling day and night.

He felt that she had killed him. It was actually worse than death; she murdered the child in him and therefore his capacity to love. He was a walking zombie without emotions and his music could not change it either.

Then he bumped into her one night, on his way home. They met under the Orion. It was only a second. Gerry did not see anything. He caught his eyes and carried on walking, but more quickly.

Leo's Defense

Leo knew that the worst thing he could have done was to fall in love with his best friend's girl, and he would breech the code of conduct they all swore to follow: We do not shoot at rabbits. Unfortunately, he knew as well that CC was the best thing he would ever meet and try his luck with. Gerry mistreated her and this made Leo love her even more, she did really deserve something better.

At the same time he felt a deep compassion for Gerry, who was so insecure that he thought it necessary to prove to the world how incredibly higher developed he was than everybody else. Girls fell for this, and Leo felt very inhibited when he was with Gerry in the company of girls. Deep inside, Leo was eternally bored with the whole human mating dance that Gerry performed with such excellence. Leo found it ridiculous that you had to astonish the chicks in order to impress them, and Gerry achieved this with all sorts of lies. He uttered these lies with such elegance; they were his second nature. As for Leo, he spent all his energy performing them. To make things worse, the attempted courtship often looked like attempted suicide. The compliments sounded untrue from his mouth, they made him even more insecure, and therefore he gave up very soon trying to lie his way into some silly girl's arms. If any of the girls found him boring that was because of their self-centered attitude, greedy-needy 'me-me-lust' for compliments and most importantly because they bored Leo. He did not want to embellish the truth to effect a better teasing; he wanted to treat them as equals. CC liked this, she liked him rough with his uneven nuances, and she remained one of the very few.

Nevertheless, Leo admired Gerry's talent and regarded him as his best friend, and strangely, in a way he was proud of him. Leo thought that his father would have wanted him to be like Gerry, but actually his father was only keen to see his academic achievements. Leo wished that his father had been more interested in real life instead of his biology and he transposed his desire of being a 'normal man,' whatever that meant, on Gerry. Leo was not normal, he was privileged. His family was pretty rich compared to the mainstream and his mates envied him for the relative freedom that he enjoyed. Leo's parents worked together, and their work involved many journeys to universities and conferences all over the world. When Leo was younger, they used to take him with on their journeys; therefore he had been to many countries in the world by the time he reached primary school. After that his grandmother used to look after him while the parents were on trips and later, when he was sixteen they trusted his common sense and intelligence so much that they let him stay on his own.

Gerry became his best friend in the college, but Leo could never find out why Gerry liked him. Leo was bullied for his spectacles and weak body; he was useless in any sport team. His best guess was that Gerry liked his musical talent. It was probably important for him, too that Leo did not question Gerry's stories about his father. Leo accepted them as true. Funnily enough, Leo was in Cairo when he was three as well, but only for a short while. He checked the dates with Gerry; they were both in Cairo approximately at the same time. Their parents might have even met. They might have played with each other in the crèche of the embassy, they just did not remember.

Leo and Lord never thought Gerry would keep on to a girl for long; this did not belong to the image of a 'grand stud.' They were truly amazed when uncharacteristically for him; Gerry seemed to have fallen in love with CC.

Leo's first impression of CC did not make her any more interesting than all the other blondes around. She was too sober for their hothead Gerry, he decided. According to his estimations their dating should have lasted for a month or so, but they stuck so intensely together that Leo even lent them his bedroom to help to ease their painful longing for each other's bodies for a short moment.

Nature was not supposed to allow them to grow old together, and as Leo and Lord had expected, Gerry pushed his luck too far. He was an adorable guy of the extremes; they had to admit that.

The meaner he treated CC, however, the more enmeshed Leo got with her. He analyzed his own feelings, suspecting that the good old protector instinct was playing the leading tunes in his lost soul, but she was too clever for a bimbo and got him by his intellect. She explained why exactly she allowed Gerry to mistreat her. It all made perfect sense to Leo, for he loved Gerry himself. Soon, the chain of events spiraled in such a fatal motion that Leo begun to feel that he was a supporting actor in a Greek tragedy.

Poisoned

At the beginning of our relationship it did not matter to me if Gerry boasted about what this or that girl gave him or wanted from him. If I felt too overwhelmed I told him some similar story from my own experience of the day or at worst invented some. It only disturbed me that he, in contrast to my generous attitude, did not show much understanding, he was even annoyed by my standing up to him.

Leo, Gerry's best friend, had become a very special friend to me, too. I liked him a great deal from the moment I first met him. His parents were doctors, and he was terribly bright himself. He was a gentle soul, a shy person gifted with wisdom. He showed lots of love and caring for all of us. I could always easily talk to him, even about Gerry and my relationship, like I could to my female friends. With him, I never experienced the barriers of the sexes, at some point I even thought he was really an angel sent to earth to look after our desperate souls.

At the beginnings I did not assume that Leo would perhaps like to date me. His friendship was too precious, and I was grateful for it, but if I expressed my feelings towards him in any way, Gerry grinned at me cynically. On the other hand, Gerry never wanted to discuss his suspicions or fears with me openly and this annoyed me. I often tried to discuss the matter, for it seemed to me that he regarded freedom as his own privilege. He always ignored my accusations and behaved as if I was trying to inflict jealousy on him.

One afternoon we all met in the Botanical Gardens and I sat down with Leo to talk. We were a little further away from the others. I saw Gerry arriving and waved to him. He didn't come to us, only smiled at me ironically from time to time.

When we joined the group, Gerry didn't greet me very warmly. He called me 'grandma,' thus I enquired:

'Are you cross with me?'

'I'd just waited one week to see you and you didn't even look at me.'

'I waved to you to come there.'

'You should have come.'

'You arrived later.'

'I didn't want to disturb you.'

'Yes, then don't disturb me any longer, OK?'

He left me alone. Leo ran after him but even he could not bring him back.

I fought against Gerry's childish sulkies for a while, until I realized that he was stronger than I was. He would leave me alone just like that, no matter where we were, and then I would not see him for even as long as a week, but that was more than unbearable. I gave in. I did not go aside if I wanted to talk to anybody and he was there. In the rare cases when he arrived later and I was already deeply involved in a conversation, I pretended not having noticed him and was silent waiting for his approach. It sounds like a huge inhibition of my freedom, but there and then I was prepared to do it, rather then wasting the preciously short time we had for us with quarrels and silly games. Surprisingly, this simple method proved sufficient to restore and keep the peace between us; therefore whenever he boasted about his real or imagined adventures with other girls I just simply smiled, thinking that they were a part of his childish pretense.

To my sadness and humility, near the end of the summer at Bangor, it came to light how cruel he could be, as he began an affair with my friend.

I had to fight hard with my parents to be allowed to go to Bangor. I took my oldest friend Aoifa with me, who had been in my class at the secondary school in Newry, my father knew her and her parents very well. The fact that she came with me calmed my parents' worries, but we had to promise to phone every day during our stay.

I still do not understand how Aoifa could betray me, when she knew how much Gerry meant to me. Perhaps he was really irresistible and sooner or later all females had to fall into his web? My boyfriend and my girlfriend cheated on me at the same time and this made me come to my senses with a big slap on the face. I had to get away from that place. When I arrived home exhausted and haunted my parents thought I had been raped, or whatever, for my mother discreetly came to my room to enquire why the weekend ended so soon. I told her that I fell out with Aoifa, which was at least part of the truth. I was embittered and wounded. The only person whom I could have told what had happened was my little sister, but I chose not to get her involved. I phoned Cathy, who had an ear for my tearful complains. Her fury about Gerry soothed my pain. While I was listening to her, I was scared to see how much inclined I was to defend him still, no matter how deeply he hurt me, I could not find in myself any hate.

'Take it as a lesson.' I tried to comfort myself. But why could I not learn to dislike him? I could not cut him off and there was nothing left for me than suffering. I loved him and found it impossible to say: 'That was it, it's all over.' Finally, I went back to him.

From that time on everything changed, however. Jealousy preyed on my mind. I knew that I was cutting the ground from under my own feet and I was even fighting for him. He was honest; he never hid his adventures from me. I could have left him any time.

I felt, however, it would have been worse if he had told lies to me. I faced a dilemma: If he could not be honest with me, there was no way for us to be friends; when he divulged his adventures, however, it was very difficult for me to regard him as my lover. Yet, I wanted to give him everything that could be given by a woman, or even by a man. I was so ambitious! A High-Flyer, yes, I was.

It added to my misery that I was deprived of almost any leave. Lying remained the solution and I was even forced to deceive my parents in order to spend time with him at weekends. I did this braving death. I wished to be together with him until we would become tired of each other, but always together. Life did not bring it so yet if the world hadn't been against it; it might have ended in the simplest way. The fire would have simply died out. In our relationship, however, I was the one, who burnt away, for I was sure, if I could be with him freely, he would not have needed anybody else.

Limits

On weekdays, if Gerry did not wait for me in front of the school, I used to go into an unpretentious Presbyterian church close to the school. My sister and I had been brought up religiously, but I had not gone to mass any longer. I always found an excuse when I was at home on Sundays, usually that I had to prepare and study. My parents accepted this argument and did not force me, except for on Christmas Day, which was fine with me, too. The celebration of the birth of the baby Jesus had never lost its special meaning for me, but I had distanced myself rapidly from the teachings of the church, since I had lost my virginity. On the other hand, I felt closer to God than ever before, for I was in love, I was love itself. I was an outcast, but with Him everywhere. Who was to say that you were only to believe if you went to church? Who had the right to say that you can only be in touch with God through such distorted transmitters like a priest or a Sister O'Hara of a convent?

At that time I was looking for my peace of mind in the church. The sacred space had a cleansing effect on me. It raised me from the every day humiliation, the hiding and lies that I was forced to commit. From time to time there were concerts in a church, or I could simply listen to the practice of the organist. These stolen hours of peace became an important part of my bleak existence.

When I was not allowed to go to a concert in the Presbyterian parish at the beginning of November I was deeply hurt and demoralized. It felt like being knifed into my side, in fact.

Sister O'Hara blew up our discussion, so that it almost became a sectarian battle. I asked her permission in the most humble manner possible for me:

'Sister O'Hara, I'd like to listen to the Requiem tomorrow afternoon. Would you please grant me a leave?'

She retorted obtusely:

'I cannot permit it, it coincides with the rehearsal.'

I was always one of the performers at every prize presentation and this would have been a rehearsal of the program.

'Yes, but who knows when I can have the opportunity to hear it again. This is in the Presbyterian Church, gratis moreover.'

'I don't know what's gone into you, Saoirse. How can you put yourself out to so much danger, haven't you heard enough about the atrocities we Catholics have to suffer in this country?'

'I've heard about the atrocities Jesus had to suffer, but they believe in Jesus, too. Somebody has to break the vicious circle we live in, and it is not written on my forehead that I am a Catholic. I'm beginning to feel that it's a burden, as much as I'm sorry for it, anyway.'

'What ignorance. We all have to make sacrifices for our faith; you cannot be an exception from that. Anyway, how can you imagine going to that church, instead of taking part in the rehearsal, when you have an important role in the prize-giving ceremony? Remember your duty, girl.'

I became very nervous and managed to make her even more furious.

'That rubbish can be read by anyone. I'm very grateful for your understanding.'

Then she began to stammer and she cancelled my leave for two weeks, in return for my disrespect.

I traveled home that weekend. In the meantime Sister O'Hara had already informed my parents. She requested them to make me see that if I would not change myself she would be compelled to suspend me for a month and that would endanger my performance at the A-level exams.

It was a long letter in which she even asked my parents to check on my circle of friends, and become certain that they approved all of them. She was afraid that it contained some hooligan elements that could only be disadvantageous for my development. I guessed she meant Gerry as they could not have seen me with anybody else in the surroundings of the convent. My father, however, needed no explanation. He immediately knew whom Sister O'Hara meant. He began an endless litany, saying that he knew people better than me, he had enough experience, and I should believe him that this boy was useless, he would never amount to anything.

'It says in this letter that your friends are irresponsible hooligans.'

'I only wanted to go to church instead of the rehearsal. That's all. That's the only reason she sent this letter.'

'Duty is the most important. I don't go to church instead of my work, either. If they tell you to celebrate then you must do as they say. And anyway, how do you dare to go to the prods' church? Have you gone mad? What if they find out that you are a Catholic? Did you cross yourself, when you went in at all?'

'Daddy, the world is very different now. Especially in Belfast. That is a huge cathedral, if you compare it to the one in Newry. Nobody cares whether I cross myself or not.'

'So. You didn't cross yourself.'

'I go there for the peace and the music that's all.'

'Now I understand. I knew that he was bad news for you. A musician and now he is a prod.'

'Daddy, this doesn't have anything to do with him. Please, believe me.'

'Saoirse, you have to forget him once and for all. I knew that he wouldn't set you a good example.'

'He is a very good boy. You know that his father is dead and his mother rears him and his brother on her own.'

I was trying to make Gerry appear pitiable; pointing out that he was a half-orphan. I thought that my father, being a religious man, could show some compassion for Gerry, if not for my sake, but for the love of Jesus. This was a hopeless endeavour. My father, who sat devotedly in the church every Sunday, became a devil if his daughters were at stake. Duty was the utmost priority for my father especially if a seventeen-year-old girl was concerned, and he was on the same wavelength with Sister O'Hara in this matter. He turned against Gerry even more; it seemed he made Gerry responsible for all the problems in the world.

'That's the point. He needs a father to knock the corners off him and whip him into shape.'

Dad was almost shouting. Mother jumped up nervously, but this time she did not come to help me. She put her hands on my shoulders, as if wanting to keep me on the earth before I flew away to escape from their loveless cage.

'Your father is right, my dear. Just imagine what it meant if you were expelled from school. We don't have the money or contacts to help you to find another place. This is the best Catholic school in Belfast. You're playing with your scholarship.'

The power of fear and the power of money were the arguments she generally used to convince me whenever I wanted to go my way.

I listened to all of this patiently then I went to bed. Mum followed me into my room. She helped me to make my bed, and then sat down on its side. She was begging me with tears in her eyes:

'Saoirse, please, don't do things like this anymore. Remember your father has a heart disease.'

I could not see in her goodness anything else than terror, and their intention to keep me well in hand to live the joyless life they had chosen for me.

My sister, Laura, could hardly wait until Mum closed the door behind herself, she was so curious. Pretending coolness, however, she casually popped the question.

'What have you done, Saoirse?'

'I wanted to go to a church. That's all.'

'How could that make Dad's heart problem worse?' she asked, revealing the naive little girl who she was in reality, but also pointing out the absurdity of the whole situation.

Though I was desperate, I had to laugh. We were laughing as confidants and were set back into the safe naughty world of our childhood for a while. I was relieved from the pressure of the fight with my parents and felt very grateful towards Laura.

'The sisters have threatened to suspend me from school, because of this. Now they have cancelled my leaves during the week.'

'Does that mean "phut" to Gerry?'

'Phut. Probably!'

'Have you had sex with him yet?'

'It's none of your business! Anyway you're too young to ask questions like that.'

My sister had to show me how mature she was, thus truly or untruly she boasted to me:

'I'm not a little girl, you know. What do you think I do with Johnny?'

'You should be careful!' I warned her and knew at the same time how careless I was myself.

'Don't talk rubbish. I know how to protect myself,' she said and left me confronted with my worries about HIV or an unwanted pregnancy.

We had made love five times by then. On the fourth and fifth occasions we were too crazy for each other and not careful. There was no reason or common sense in our encounters. We did not talk much about contraception with Gerry. I did try to get a prescription for the pill from Dr Murphy, our family GP, but she refused me. She simply said I was too young for that, not yet eighteen. I told her that the age of consent is seventeen in Northern Ireland, but she was rigid with her opinion. From that time on I was also worried that she might tell my mother about my request.

I switched off the light and ordered my sister to be silent and let me sleep. I could not do so, however, I had to think about my parents. I had the same wish again that I had had for some years then: to be eighteen. But I knew deep within me that I would not change my attitude towards them very much, because I always felt pity for them.

I saw that it was terribly difficult to bring up a child. Even if the parents had set off with the most honesty and integrity, they both had to have strength to resist the conventions that informed their own childhood. Why did all the parents I knew have to replay the same old songs, I did not know? Why did they have to become the embodiments of all those qualities that they hated in their own parents as youngsters? The world believes that growing up means rigidity and losing trust. I firmly vowed to myself that I would never allow the past to cast its shadows into my future. Never.

With this curtain raiser, of course, I did not have a chance to get away from home during the weekends either. I was waiting for the winter holidays and for New Year's Eve when we had a chance to meet again. I was cautious not to mention Gerry at all, but my father was on the alert and forbade me to spend New Year's Eve with Orla in Lurgan. After Christmas I was allowed to go to see her, but I was told to come home with the last train. Orla had a grand house party, for Auntie Louise and Uncle John went away. We waited until the last train's departure time. Then Orla phoned my parents to tell them that I missed the last train, and I asked them to allow me to stay overnight. We pleaded and begged so effectively that they could not say 'no.'

I spent that night with Gerry. I was happy to be able to sleep with him after such a long time and I did!

We had to stay in the darkness in order not to wake his mother and his brother, Liam. Only the snow shone through the window. It was dreadfully cold, but I was not able to wait until we grew warm with kisses. I just needed him in me, his heat spreading out in me. It was dark, but I could see in his eyes as he was approaching me, removing light-years of distance. When he arrived, I was crushed; I did not exist anymore.

My parents received me with surprising understanding and kindness. Nevertheless, I was too frightened to sneak out from home on New Year's Eve.

I met Gerry in the first week of January again. He told me quietly that he spent New Year's Eve with another girl. I did not ask him what had happened. It was all too obvious to me. Yet this infidelity knocked me down. I could not understand how it was possible for him to step over the memory of that night so easily. I knew that he loved me, then how could he be with some other girl?

On the first day of school after the winter break he was waiting for me in front of the school building. He was standing there, innocently as if nothing had happened, but I did not kiss him. I felt cold suddenly. I wanted to punish this careless child for his ignorant cruelty. He said that love and sex were different things, but they had never been with me.

Escape

We parted, but not for long. He was there again. It seemed he had never ever gone away. We went together to the cinema, theatre, and concerts.

My pain revolted only in the depth of my soul, for we were only friends on the surface. He continued writing me letters and I was fair enough to answer. I loved him terribly and knew it would not take long, all my jealous fears and sufferings would start from the beginning. I could not bring up the energy to face them again, I felt old and broken.

In the middle of February, when I was forced to suspect that I was pregnant, I got dreadfully scared. I imagined my parents' faces when I told them that I was to have a baby out of wedlock, I thought my father would have a heart attack, as my mother had warned me. And herself, my mother would be so ashamed of me. The daughter of the high school's principle having a baby unmarried. Unheard! The ridicule of town.

I lost my trust in the relationship with Gerry, and I felt sure that if I kept the baby I would be alone in the world. I regarded my relationship with Gerry for finished, but his letters obliged me to inform him at least. It did not even occur to me to ask his advice. I believed this responsibility to be mine in the first place; thus I was the one who had to decide. All the arguments were against the baby. Why have children from a boy whom you cannot trust? I had my plans of study. Literature would be my true love. That would make me happy!

One night I was tossing around in my bed, crying in my dreams. Laura woke me and I told her that I was pregnant. She helped me. My sixteen-year-old 'little' sister kept the telephone number of an organization in England 'just in case' that was advertised in a newspaper. I called them the next day and they booked me into a clinic in Liverpool. I had two weeks left to find seven hundred pounds for the trip.

When I told my friends at the college what I was planning, Sylvia could not stop her mouth and slipped that only Protestants have abortions, but Cathy immediately took my side and assured me of her full support. The following days they really did everything to get me money; they sold most of their valuable things, even the CD-player.

I started the day with vomiting most mornings. My friends looked after me; they treated me like a sick child, or rather like an insane child, comforting me with the prospect that I would be 'cured' very soon. Sylvia taught me to put make-up on, what I never did before, to cover my paleness that would have given rise to suspicion. I had to struggle very hard not to be discovered in the college and I felt guilty for being pregnant, just as much as for planning to get rid of it. I was deeply sunk in sin, no doubt.

The weight of this secret was so enormous to bear. I knew that I had to tell Gerry, even if it hurt. I had to be honest at least with him. My soul was expecting an operation, if it succeeded, I would be saved. The love I felt for him pressed down on me so much that I could hardly manage to breathe. I was hoping to get free, but I could not suspect that freedom would be so hard to bear.

Gerry did not support my decision in any form, he even begged me to keep the baby, but it was too late. I did not believe him.

I scraped together my savings for a Spanish holiday I planned for the time after my eighteenth birthday and sold my golden bracelet and a necklace with a cross that I got for my Communion. With the eighty-nine pounds so generously provided by my friends, still, I only had five hundred and ten. Then braving death I asked my father for money. I explained to him that I planned to go to England to see Liana, an old school friend of mine, who moved there with her father a couple of years before. My father seemed to startle for a minute or so, then he gave me three hundred without any further questions. Later I found his friend's address on my desk. Dr Kennedy was the name on the business card and when I read it I started shaking. I had no idea whether my father knew why I was going to Liverpool; did he guess my trouble? I felt deeply embarrassed by the thought that he might know my secret.

I flew over to Liverpool, stayed at my friend Liana's. She was very kind and supportive, but she did not agree with my decision. She came with me to the woman's clinic and cried her eyes out while she was waiting.

The clinic was in a red brick house in a block of red brick houses. I've never seen so much red in a street ever before. It all seemed unreal and exaggerated. Everything was well organized, sterile and exact, but I felt that everybody looked at me strangely. Only an older woman showed some sympathy for me. She was moaning after the operation deliriously. She asked me remotely, she had to shout, and she was so lost in the mist of her pain:

'Do you know what you are doing?'

I did not reply, the nurse was calling my name. She wore rubber gloves. I was given an injection and within seconds I was hovering on grey clouds, a part of me watching indifferently what was done to my body. She led me into a modern operating-hall. The white walls were hidden in semi-darkness. There was a light in the middle pointing at the gynecologist's chair, bloody bins around. An old doctor was washing his hands in the corner, *Like Pilate*, I thought, but he did not say the famous words. He said instead:

'There is no reason to be worried, we will be finishing soon.'

When I was lying on the operation chair, tied down, with my wide-open legs, I felt my heart being sucked out with precise attention, but this heart was dead already. Nobody's humiliating behavior could ever hurt it again.

In that moment I did not care whether the world had contempt for me. I had made up my mind; I could not change it anymore. I got into the airplane and there was nothing more to be afraid of. It would either crash halfway or land in a completely different world. Either or, it was all beyond my control.

Gerry, being faithful to his promise, broke off our relationship. He did not spare me. He called me a murderer which was not far from the truth. Nevertheless, I sighed: 'That was it. It's over.'

Free?

Though they had become indifferent to me, I occupied myself with the tedious pursuit of my aims. I learnt and learnt. Consequently, I was admitted to university. My last months in the convent were spent in near isolation. People said I was my own shadow. I retreated completely. Everybody, even my parents attributed this change to Gerry, but I cut them short if they questioned me. There was nothing to explain; I did not comprehend the bygone events myself. For some inexplicable reason I felt a loss inside me that I buried as deeply as I could. I made myself believe that this way I would be able to function in my everyday life, with success.

The only task I could not tackle was to put on a cheerful mask, although I tried it very hard. With time's passing, however, I looked back at the operation with growing disconcert and doubt. My emptiness seemed to be the result of my cowardice and I always hated half-hearted people. I began to think that I had pushed away my happiness with both hands, because I was unable to forgive Gerry and eventually I was not capable to love.

I not only had this negative opinion of myself, but I also disliked my parents. My mother must have sensed the change in me, for she turned against me. She kept criticizing everything I did. Her scorn was burning my skin, and I took it as an expression of her disgust over that what I did. Over my sin. She must have seen that I was a sinner. She must have sensed that my sudden growing up and becoming a woman had something evil about it, hence I fell for a man, let his passion overwhelm me, so that I allowed him to abuse me, and eventually, I killed his baby in my womb. I fell from her saintly mother's paradise; I lost my innocence forever. Hate shocked me, but I had nothing left for her or for myself. The world was dead, like an aborted embryo.

Where was my great love, literature? I participated mechanically in the lectures, though my dream had come true. I watched myself with contempt. The student of literature, who was ardently analyzing the great thoughts of mankind, while her heart was a dry well that swallowed all human emotions, without giving back anything.

I discovered a warning in each piece of written work. They all talked about feelings as the most valuable treasures in one's life that should be protected and cared for appropriately.

I developed anorexia and stopped eating for days. Nobody noticed my new habit of self-destruction, and I was wasting away slowly and continually.

Leo tried to pull me back into his world of light and love and invited me to their cottage in Bangor in the autumn. We were sitting at the veranda, and I saw Gerry's face in every corner. I felt his kiss on my neck.

Leo was very happy, and I knew I was not fair with him, when I let him struggle for me in vain:

'While we meditate we unite with the silence inside us. Then we recognize the light in ourselves, which is God. I've already tried it a couple of times. But it's hard to achieve a state of mind in which you don't think of anything. At the beginning it was hard, but then I learnt to relax. I'd never thought that you had to learn it, but it's true. You can breathe yourself into relaxation. This is a fantastic new world. Would you like me to teach you?'

He was looking at me without realizing that I had not been listening. I was not there at all. I was in the desert far away; a Bedouin prince was riding a camel on the horizon, towards me. I was singing a serpent melody. I was dancing with the wind.

My parents liked Leo. Once he came to see me in Newry and they invited him to stay for dinner. Leo and my father understood each other well. They enjoyed talking about religion. My father even tried to sell me to him:

'We always lived a very religious life. Marriage is holy for us just as the union of man and woman. We follow the same doctrine that the Church professes: we must accept what God gives us. If He wants us to have another child we will want His will.'

Leo was nodding with an enthusiastic expression on his face. Only Laura discovered that I was struggling with my tears. I hated my father for being two-faced, for having silently supported me and now lying so piously to my friend. Poor Leo was blind in his eager love for me; he had no idea how far he catapulted himself from me in that second of communion in my father's lies.

'Well, my son, if you have serious intentions, don't forget this: We live in the face of God.'

I was cross with my father, but I could not show it. I swallowed my anger feeling a perverse pleasure when it got down into my empty stomach, the size of a walnut. I imagined my dead body thinned to the bones, being discovered by my father one morning. *That will teach him*, I thought, *then I will laugh*. The next moment, old sensible Saoirse took over once again. I knew very well that my father was concerned about me, and that he always wanted the best for me in his strange and mostly antagonistic way, just like he did when he gave me the money to go to Liverpool. Liverpool—a pool of blood. I saw myself swimming in it. I heard my own estranged voice, saying it aloud:

'A pool of blood.'

Everybody looked at me surprised. I saw with great satisfaction a spark of scare in Dad's eyes. Laura was so shocked that she had to cover her mouth in order to keep a cry inside.

With all the attention directed on me I stood up and reminded Leo that he had to catch his train.

Confused and Lost

I began to go to Lurgan frequently, in the hope of seeing Gerry. I believed if I could look into his eyes once again I could wake up from this nightmare. His words, when he said that I killed love, were still echoing in my ears. I wanted to be assured that I had not killed anything or anybody.

I never found him there, but I spent some time with his mother on each occasion, who told me that he had been very close to suspension from his school at the end of November. He was supposed to sleep at home, but often stayed at his friend's place in Belfast.

Mrs. Tanner told me stories about their time in Cairo when Gerry's father was alive. It was strange to hear them from her, as I had never been sure about the truth behind these tales when I had heard them from Gerry. They sounded like a dream: he in the desert sand, playing with Arabian children, yellow sun, heat, pyramids, women in veils, and the music. I think I was like all of his friends: I did not dare to express my doubts for I did not want to hurt him, but I did not believe them, either. Having heard the story from his mother, the picture that I had of him transformed instantly, too. I realized that he had never lied to me; therefore he must have meant it honestly when he pleaded me to keep the baby. I felt so ashamed. I longed to see him more feverishly than ever before.

I left letters there, in one of them I suggested playfully a meeting at the feet of the pyramids, but he returned them to me unopened. I never got a reply.

A new year started again. At the beginning of January, not long after my empty and meaningless New Year's Eve party my wish came true.

I left their house at about nine in the evening, to catch the last train back to Belfast, where I lived in a rented room during terms. It was chillingly cold. Here and there ice-crystals were falling from the sky. No soul was in the streets. I hurried, in order not to be cold and scared. I played some old music in my head.

I stopped at a road, for I heard the noise of an engine. I looked to the other side. Gerry was standing there. He looked at me, and his sharp indifference struck me. It was just a glimpse but sufficient.

The car passed, we continued on our ways both in our own directions. He was speeding to get away. I was staggering. An eternity passed before I managed to cross the road and reached the other side. I looked up to the stars with great effort, as if I was fighting against some viscous medium. They were very near, though very far away. There was the empty space between us that seemed to be dominating everything. I was alone. Everything around me, the road, the barrier, the bare trees were swimming in an unreal light. That glimpse remained the only reality. Staying there by the road, I gathered myself to look into his heart with my mind's eyes once again. I was able to feel what he felt, and suddenly I shared his hate for me. I had not had the strength to trust him, and my love, if it had ever existed, was too weak. It was clear as the crystal night: I failed. My life was worthless. I was lost in darkness; the last silver cord to light was ripped from my being.

The cruelty of this revelation stripped my soul in a second and pushed me into icy despair. The sudden intensity of feelings shocked me after the long-lasting apathy that had almost become my second nature. I was not able to put up with myself anymore. I was trapped in the Hell of my own emotions, guilt, pain; shame built a dark wall around me. I knew that I either had to die or get help.

My nineteenth birthday was celebrated in a forced atmosphere at home. I felt that everybody was watching me and I had to pretend that I was happy with the presents, and the cake. My eyes were wandering around in the room, trying not to stop on anything or anybody. Then all of a sudden I realized that the statue of Mary has been looking at me all along. Her stupid look full of goodness and compassion turned my stomach upside down. I felt an impulse to go there and knock her over, but I did not move. Good old Saoirse gained control over the uprising emotions once again. Now I could see her clearly. She behaved very much like Miss O'Hara, our headmistress. I hated her more than ever before.

Leo was there with us. He tried it for a last time; he presented me with a ring. My sister jumped there, to see the dream of every girl: an engagement ring. I was embarrassed, my parents terribly joyous. My cut out baby started to ache in my belly. I had to put an end to this theatre.

I went with Leo to the station, to give back the ring. He did not say a word, he was hurt.

Back in the house, avoiding Mary's eyes, I thanked my mother for everything. She asked me not to forget to switch off the heating after having had my bath. I did not put it on at all. The bath got wadded with steam within seconds. I slipped into the hot water and sunk under the surface, waiting for death to come and take me.

It was an unfair game. I went down, giving in, and the life force or the instincts brought me up again. Then I searched through the little medicine case that was hanging on the wall next to the mirror, and found my father's old razor. Suddenly I was active and fully aware of my power. I cut my left wrist. It was like banging a door behind me. It was nothing in comparison to the abortion, which was more like banging the door in front of Gerry. This time it was only my body.

For an endless time I felt nothing but pain. My blood painted the bath red and I started to feel weaker by the minute. In a flash of a second a force dragged me to my funeral. I watched the suffering of my family. I could feel their pain much stronger than anything ever before. I could not escape into apathy, however, this was different. I had to watch and feel. My mother broken down, crying, my father grayed overnight, awkwardly fighting to hold my mother while in thoughts feeling utterly guilty, and Laura lonely and isolated, left alone with her fears and doubts about life. I realized that not trust was that I lost, but the opportunity to learn to love again.

Suddenly I was wide-awake. I grabbed my bleeding wrist, wrapped it into a towel, pulled my knitted dress on, and rushed into my bedroom, where Laura was still awake. I asked her to help. She put a tie on my upper arm and called a taxi on her mobile. While we were waiting she pulled some clothes on me, helped me to put my shoes on and covered my back with a blanket, for I started to feel very cold and weak. When the taxi arrived we sneaked through the window.

It was chillingly cold outside! We were rushed to the hospital, where I was treated in the Casualty. The doctor said that he needed to keep me there for the night, for I had lost too much blood. He phoned my parents. They arrived later that night, when I was already hospitalized at the ward. I was lying on a wheeled bed, blood dripping into my right arm from a red pipe. I remember seeing my father standing at the end of the bed, wavering like a shadow of himself, sad and helpless. I felt ashamed and terribly lost, but I could not tell him any of that.

Martina

The futile attempt to escape from my pain by trying to leave this world opened a new chapter in my life. I had counseling after my suicide attempt. It was the starting point of a long process, in which I gained trust and appreciation for myself. I was allowed to face my pain and pour it out in front of a person who was totally uninvolved in my life. When I saw the disgusting debris of my life my first impulse was to hide, cover up my wound and try to live a normal life. With the help of that counselor I saw, however, that by doing so I would repeat the same pattern that I fell into after the abortion. There had to be another way, it was no longer good enough to sweep everything under the carpet, and to pretend that nothing happened to me. It took me a long time to understand that the life force was much stronger in me than any depression and indeed, I gave myself a new chance to change my life. I was on a significant journey from darkness to light.

In the counseling centre I found the phone number of a psychotherapist, Martina. I do not know what drew me to her, it was a leap of faith, but it was worthwhile. She offered to treat me with hypnotherapy, and I found a friend in her.

Hypnosis was an amazing discovery, for I realized how deeply connected I was to the field hidden under and beyond everything. I saw that I had been into this land before, when

I tried to meditate in the way as Leo explained to me, and when I emptied myself for Gerry's call in our synchronicity game.

Martina took me to journeys within myself, and I always returned with a new revelation, like the pearl diver that returns to the surface with yet another gem. I should be very grateful to Martina, for she saved my life, but she is telling me that I am the one who does the healing, when I open myself to the great love I carry inside.

It was not easy to open myself. At the beginning it was very painful, for I had to trust her and myself and trust was the very quality I had lost. I also felt responsible for Gerry's misery and for his hostility, and I carried the weight of guilt on many different layers of my inner world.

It seemed that I was wandering in cold darkness. I could only see a tiny beam of light around the edges of my perception and I followed that. I was still alone. It felt as if I had died, anyway, it was even darker and colder than I had ever felt in life. I wanted to fall asleep and dream that I am alive. There was no sleep, only bothering thoughts and fear.

Whenever I despaired, Martina was there for me. We talked about guilt and shame. I could see that the space I created for myself with my destructive emotions materialized in the cold and dark I experienced during my journeys under hypnosis. With her help I understood that these feelings had been planted into my subconscious through my upbringing and the fact that I could not share my problem with anybody else.

I did a lot of research into abortion. Having lived it through with body and soul, I was trying to understand it with my mind and to gain some distance from it. I found out that it has been done for thousands of years and in some eastern cultures it was part of the job of the midwife, just as much as helping babies into the world. Of course in those countries, death is naturally an everyday matter, an important part of life. They believe in reincarnation, therefore death is only transition. People try to die consciously; they want to take a pure soul into their next lives. They walk over smoothly, then either stay in Nirvana forever, or slip into another body. In the west we cling so forcibly to life that it becomes necessary for death to cut us off with his scythe. Then we either fall into Hell or go to Heaven.

Although there can never be scientific evidence to support it, psychics say that the soul only settles down in the body in the seventh month of pregnancy. During the first six months it enters and leaves the body by its own choice, as it feels like. It often happens that the soul decides to give away the body to another soul, if urgency or the conditions of life would be more appropriate for the later arrived. The most amazing wisdom I learnt from these books was the idea that we all chose our experiences, we even chose our parents. So, during this initial settling time a fully conscious woman should be able to explain to the soul that its coming is not timely, and in such a case miscarriage could happen naturally.

My choice of having an abortion was very conscious, but it came from misplaced intentions. In reality I loved that baby a lot, but I lost trust in Gerry and I was not strong enough to have it on my own. When I decided to cut the ties to Gerry in the form of the baby, I exchanged my love for longing and that empty longing caused all my pain.

My visits to the other side became frequent and easier with each hypnotherapy session. After a timeless period spent in the cold, a transparent, yet very bright being, reminiscent of a little fairy flew to me. I recognized the soul who had been around me once before, during my pregnancy. After playfully fluttering around my head for a while, it settled down on my chest and only then could I see that the glistening light that I had been following originated from there. It came from my heart. All of a sudden, I felt so light! I was filled with forgiveness.

It was the most wonderful gift, being able to meet this tiny, yet infinite soul. I knew that the time would come when we could live together as mother and child. On the other hand, it was telling me that love is love, no matter what form it takes and we could be friends or sisters, or husband and wife, or grandmother and grandchild, the lesson would be the same, learning to love without limitations. It talked in a wordless language, about being fully in the present and that the past and the future were not real, they were the longing of the present to be something else.

I felt liberated for the first time in my long recovery. We talked about the importance of caring for each other and that through my experience I could help other people, women and men who suffer because of having made a 'bad' choice. It was as if that little soul had given me the task to make these people aware of the truth. I have to tell everybody that we choose our experiences, and when we apparently make the 'bad' choice it is still 'good,' for its consequences help us to grow. I decided to study psychotherapy. I also took up voluntary work at the Brook Centre in Belfast, where I could help girls and boys to deal with the responsibility that accompanies sexual adulthood.

With Martina's help I have traveled around the earth many times. As I was getting better, my light grew and grew. I often visited the desert and saw Gerry, but he could not see me. He was covered with some mist or white smoke. We could not communicate, for he was too much sunken into his own world and padded himself with drugs, but I knew he often felt me being around.

I still travel in my dreams, and these experiences permeate my whole being. The desert calls me. Gerry always appears on the horizon, on the top of a sand wave. The wheels of the motorbike spray the sand around. Very slowly, with each new encounter he surfs closer to me. When he arrives I show him our baby. He is perplexed, but flashes a gentle smile.

Then something stops me. I suddenly understand that I have no right to keep him there with us and I have to make him aware of this with as much compassion as I am capable to give:

'You always have a choice, Gerry. You can go back, do you know?'

The dream recurs like an old record, and I think it will do so, until he makes up his mind.

Leo's Journey

There were moments when Leo loved CC and Gerry with the same intensity and this confused him even more. Was he bisexual, or even gay?

If he wanted to be honest, he had to admit that he was frightened to find out the truth. He'd rather search somewhere else. He was chasing himself into pretty girls' laps, while he was disgusted by his own cowardice. Gerry's loyalty and his palish endeavors to help him pushed Leo even further away, but it also made him realize that he loved Gerry, more than he wanted to admit.

Of course, this was ridiculous. You can not love more or less, you love or you do not love. Love is a spiritual experience, Leo told himself, but he could not get rid of the idea of loving Gerry in a more earthbound, erotic way. He prayed and he believed that God saved him from touching Gerry, though. No, he did never think of wanting to touch him, but he wanted to unite with him in such a way that would transform them, like the ecstasy of love.

Playing music with Gerry had always been a similarly metaphysical experience and there they were free to express anything. Their gender did not put up a barricade between them. It was very strange, but true that after Gerry and CC split up, the band's orchestral work changed, too. It became mechanical; Gerry was not there at all. Leo could not make love with him through musical improvisations, the game of composing or just performing together cadences and accords, lyrics and songs.

When Leo realized that Gerry had lost his soul, he tried to find out from Gerry what had happened. Gerry had no answer, but Lord made Leo understand that Gerry was on drugs. What could they do? They could not call the police or a doctor. Gerry had total authority over his own life and he was the only one having the power to change it. His friends just watched him losing control, standing by, ready to catch him when he fell, hoping that if they failed him, once he reached the bottom he would not break his bones, but wake up with a blow.

While Gerry was on his trips to nowhere Leo was left alone with his confusions. Suspecting that CC held the key to all their sufferings, and the magic wand to heal them all with a single wave of it, he ran to her hoping for a miracle.

Of course, she was just as broke as Gerry or Leo. It rather seemed that she needed Leo's help, which he gave her with all his heart. But sex? Was Leo really so bad in sending messages to the other sex? She never ever touched Leo, neither did he touch her, and they never kissed. Sometimes, arriving home after an exhausting date with her Leo hated himself so much, for not being taken seriously. He suffered. The possibility of being gay made his knees soft, and transformed his father's image in his head into a dragon.

His intellect, to start with, was excited roused and inspired by her from the first minutes he got to know her. When she sent him off Leo felt hurt, but just as relieved for some reason. He did not have to prove anymore what a great guy he was. He crawled into a corner to lick his wounds. She approached him about six months later again. She was there with her sensual voice at the other end of the line. Leo started to play the piano for her on the phone and they also went out a few times.

Saoirse told Leo that she was having psychotherapy sessions and this made him curious. She recounted her journeys during hypnoses and Leo suddenly realized that she visited the same planes of reality that he did, during his meditations.

Very often, when Leo mastered the preliminary state of calming his thoughts and sunk into not thinking he found himself in places he never saw before. Ethereal places, we could say, where lights and shades of colors were floating in the air, like mobile building blocks ever changing, always transforming into something else.

Leo often saw Gandhi, the greatest altruist of the twentieth century. He was riding about, sometimes on the back of a horse, sometimes on a motorbike.

Once the great spirit of Gandhi stopped in front of Leo. He had gleeful eyes and his bold head was shining in the sun emanating waves of light, like the tall flames of a torch. He said: The truth is in you.

His voice echoed deafening Leo with its power. The sound whipped up a storm, whirling and spiraling around him. Leo felt trapped in the eye of the cyclone, desperately stirred up but lame, waiting to be spit out at the other end of the whirl that seemed to be so totally indefinite.

Yes, he knew the truth was inside him, but where exactly? Hopefully not in his neglected penis that only seemed to rise when he smelled the sweat loaded damp vapors after PE in the boys changing room at the school.

Leo practiced meditation searching for God. Instead of Him he often saw CC and Gerry, like dancing shadows over the horizon. This was a shock, like a slap into the face. First he was inclined to hear the Devil laughing in the background. He could even see his dark and ugly face, his lips pulled into a winning smile, in the corners blood dripping. The whole experience scared him so much that he was close to a nervous breakdown. Leo thought that he was dying and the Devil was going to take his soul. He dragged himself out of the meditation.

He thought he was lucky, for his parents were abroad. Otherwise, he might have broken down in the arms of his mother confessing his filthy thoughts and that he was in love with a girl and a boy. Instead of that Leo was running about like a madman, nervously sensing icy cold winds blowing from Church doors.

CC was the only person with whom he could have shared this experience. After days spent in agony he phoned her. She had the simplest and most astonishing answer to Leo's nightmare:

'There is nothing wrong with love. The Devil cannot take you as long as you still have a drop of it in your soul. Go back and ask him what he wants.'

How could she say that? She was a sinner herself, she had an abortion and tried to kill herself, but she was right. She was indeed a true sorceress. Deep inside Leo knew himself that there was no way back, for the desert was in him. No matter how far he wanted to run from it he still would have carried the entrance in himself. Running away did not make any sense. If there was a Devil he had to face him, it was the Devil in his own being that he had to face. He prepared himself for the big jump into the void. He agreed with himself that he would accept whatever the outcome. This was to be his initiation.

Fate

CC died for Gerry when she aborted their baby. She left a huge black hole behind, nastily stinking to heaven. Gerry felt like running, living life as rapidly as possible. Yet time was jolting.

He tried to heal himself with every kind of remedy, with sex above all, but as soon as he discovered that a girl started to fall in love with him, he was leaving.

There were good things, however, especially the music. He started the day by playing the drums every morning, directing his attention to the outside; he did his best to show the world noisily that he was alive. If the world believed him, perhaps he could believe in it, too. When he felt that he was losing his heightened energy and it was to be feared that pain would steal itself into the silence, he cheered himself up with some music again. It was always nice to see a shade of horror on the indifferent faces around him, when he let himself go in some public place, in a café or the train station.

Needless to say, except for his brother Liam, nobody was able to stay near him for long. He would have left himself alone as well, if he could. When he smoke the first cigarette filled with 'angel dust' at the back of the railway station, he thought he was going to explode and that would have been all right with him. But instead of an explosion, a buzzing came over him, the grin spread out on his face by itself. For a moment, but only for a moment, he didn't have to be afraid of his own emptiness. Sweet melancholy, an extended orgasm, the heat of Cairo filled him. For about half an hour the world was in harmony with Gerry, there was peace inside and outside. He did not feel the pain about Fergus, the baby, CC or his father; they all resided in their due place in Heaven instead of maliciously haunting him in Hell. When the thirty minutes numbness was gone, he was there again in his reality, naked to the bones, whirling in pain and exhausted.

Gerry knew so many people, though there was no one who had really known him. Nobody liked him, for he often lied and laughed at people, if they believed him. Why to be honest if there was no remedy for the pain that it caused?

Gerry consciously chased away his friends. Leo stopped talking to him; Lord was the last one to stay. Gerry got rid of him as well and he did it in an utterly humiliating way, by using a girl Lord fancied.

Gerry was really fed up with himself, too, but he felt that there was no rescuing love, no forgiveness for him. He had no explanation for his behavior, except his own conceited superiority: Anybody who had a brain left him alone and he left alone those who had none.

New Year's Eve was a consolation for him. Leo and Lord organized a jam session with almost fifteen other musicians at Billy's Club and he got an invitation. He thought that his music was indispensable, but in reality his friends had pity on him and were trying to save him from further damaging himself.

There were at least a hundred people in the club, enjoying the music. Gerry saw so many blond girls among them; this filled him with painful melancholy. He crashed out after that. He had a blackout for months, possibly years, he could not tell anymore. Time lost its meaning. Then it was springtime again.

A Call

One morning, but it could have been afternoon, as far as he was aware, Gerry got up after a long and dreamless sleep. Still half-awake he started practicing his clarinet. Music was his lifeline, the only thing that could keep him in this reality. Then, in the middle of an improvised tune, with an electric shock, he felt CC calling inside him. His whole being was widely open to the sound of that call, chanting a high-pitched cry, like singing whales in the ocean. All the strings of his body where resonating with this melody. He jumped on his bike and started off.

He only reckoned later, how strange it was that he did not have any doubts, not even for a second. There was no sense for the reality inside him; he did not consider that a girl who had betrayed and left him more than two years before could not possibly call. She was dead for him, after all.

When he got on the bike he could feel her presence, she was kissing him, and she slid her smooth fingers under his shirt. Gerry drove to the river. The Lagan showed no signs of change; it carried its brown and dirty mass along as always, flowing indifferently in front of his feet. He did not know what to do; the urge to be united with her was still there. He sat back on the bike and drove on slowly, until he arrived to the railway crossing. The light showed green. Gerry stopped amazed. It was her message! It meant that he was free.

All of a sudden, Gerry did not feel the need to prove that he could go anywhere. It was just a simple truth. He stopped at green. Gerry felt that in that second, on making that decision he became a man. He stepped over into manhood, witnessed by her soul.

There was no one in his life that he could share this experience with. It was the secret between him and CC. He watched the green lights, humming a blues in his head, the one he played for CC in the schoolyard the first time they met.

On his way home, he could still feel her intriguing presence in his pocket. He was happy.

With this clandestine meeting a new era started in Gerry's life. He frequently met CC in dreams.

Once, in a dream about riding a camel in the desert, he recognized how freedom physically felt. He was the genuine Prince from Cairo. His hair was waving in the wind in rhythm with the camel's oceanic motions. CC was sitting behind him and she laughed and laughed.

When he woke up the following morning, he knew that CC had forgiven him and she was waiting for him somewhere. It could be only a step before they would be together again, but there was no way they could have forced it, their reunion had to happen in its own time and through synchronicity.

Gerry got up and cleared all the stuff out of his life. He washed all his drugs down the loo, and then he went to find his mother, who was making breakfast in the kitchen.

With a passionate upsurge of emotion he kissed her all over.

'Are you mad, you'll knock me over,' Marie said, laughing.

'Oh, Mum, something wonderful happened.'

'Are you in love again?' she asked hopefully.

'No. I can feel a presence in everything.'

'What presence?'

'I don't know. It's a strong force I can feel in everything. It's deeply connecting.'

Marie was amazed by the sudden enlightenment of her son.

'Gerry, that force is God.'

'Now I know what it means. This force knows whatever it does to people. We should be grateful whatever happened.'

He was not sure whether she understood, or whether he himself really knew what he was talking about, but he needed a point of connection with his mother. Gerry was filled with compassion for Marie's sadness about his dad's departure and he tried to ease her deep-seated pain.

'I know, darling. Thank you,' she said, surprising him again, as if she had read his thoughts.

Although Marie was happy that Gerry discovered God, she became deeply concerned at the same time. Something was very wrong and the fact that God showed Himself to Gerry gave her a strong foreboding of death.

Gerry held her in his arms for a while. He had the prickles of presentiment in his veins again, and he knew that he had to prepare her for something serious. Having polished his soul with love and gratitude, he knew he was ready for the last ride.

Desert

Liam had to watch his brother's suffering, his sinking in that pit of mad love he fell into with Saoirse.

Other members of the family were concerned about their intense feelings, too, especially their grandparents in Belfast, when they spent the last part of the winter holidays with them.

Liam loved his grandmother. She was a strong woman, she spread her love with her whole body and behavior, there were no edges around her, and she was so fluent like the milk with honey she used to make for 'her boys.' Even the loud quarrels were played with a constant smile in the corners of her eyes.

They used to spend their days watching the telly when they were in Belfast. On rare occasions Liam went outside to play with the neighbors' children, but he did not like them. He did not like throwing stones and jumping up and down from fences. The cemetery was also very close and Liam felt the heavy weight of mourning in the air, not to mention the funeral marches that interrupted their games from time to time. Liam felt safer inside the house with his Grannies.

Gerry went to town sometimes, to meet Leo, but he was a Protestant and lived somewhere near the university, in a beautiful terraced house. Whenever he went out the grannies were worried till he came back, but the most entertaining, constant excitement was caused by Gerry getting a letter one day. The grandparents did not have a computer and clearly, Gerry and Saoirse decided to use snail mail, just to be together in some form again. He also used to write to CC twice daily, which was accompanied by nagging comments by their granny.

Gerry and Granddad were playing chess one afternoon in the winter holidays between Christmas and New Year's Eve. Their grandmother came in. Dressed in her conventional apron, she had just interrupted her work in the kitchen. In one hand she was holding a wooden spoon that looked like a smoking torch, in her other hand she was waving a letter that Gerry had been waiting for all morning.

'You've only arrived and we are being flooded with letters. Have you got a new girlfriend? Sonny, don't chase the true love, she'll come your way anyway. Am I right, Sean?'

Their grandfather was just grumbling as always:

'Yeah, yeah, but don't disturb the kid, Molly, it's his turn.'

Gerry made a move as he was told, but concentrated on his grandmother:

'Why do you keep holding that letter, Gran?'

'You'll get it when you give me your jeans. It's time to wash them.'

'Hah! What a passionate woman!'

They all laughed like silly goats. Gerry took off his trousers and made her happy with them. He got the letter in return, but he pointed out:

'It's blackmail, what you're doing.'

Granddad comforted Gerry:

'She does the same with me. Women! They always get what they want. You'll find that out soon for yourselves.'

Suddenly it was three of them poor men against the powerful matriarch, and Liam felt being torn between the lines, reluctant to take sides.

'Hah, hah,' Gerry said theatrically, and opened CC's letter. He sunk into it immediately, leaving Liam to sort out the eternal fight between the genders. However, the worry about Gerry united his grannies immediately; they looked at each other surprised. Liam guessed that they had never had time for so much passion when they were young or they just did not have so much imagination. After a minute full of tension, Gerry started to shout and gesticulate angrily, jumping up and down in his underpants:

'I'll kill that man. He doesn't allow her to celebrate New Year's Eve with me. And she obeys. How can an almost eighteen-year-old woman be her parents' slave?'

Granny looked at Gerry as if he had already killed his would-be father-in-law, while Granddad was standing there as God's index finger, full of threatening admonition.

'Life is full of disappointments. You can be sure it won't be the last one.'

The darkness of these words echoed in Liam's ears when he saw Gerry crying on his bed a few months later.

'Gerry, what happened?' he asked his bro concerned. He had not seen him crying for years. Gerry pulled himself together to be the big brother he was, with little success.

'CC had an abortion and she is dead,' he said. Liam was thoroughly shocked and felt deep sorrow for Gerry and from this moment on he did not move from his side. He watched him spiraling down into destruction, noticing that he started taking drugs, too. Liam followed him everywhere, like a watchdog, though it was very difficult to be with him, for he embarrassed his little brother many times.

One afternoon they were hanging out in their favorite youth club in Lurgan. Gerry was with a girl called Judy, who was his girlfriend in charge, one in a long procession. Lord was trying to pick up a newcomer girl, Susan, a German exchange student, who just arrived from her home country. She made a very sound and sober impression. She was blond and had a perfect figure; she was wearing a knitted dress that outlined the shape of her breasts. It was obvious that Lord fancied her, his excitement was almost tactile in the air. Listening to his courting, Gerry must have got bored, for he picked up a wooden fife that was lying on the table, Lord's handy-work. Judy was caressing his shoulder.

Susan looked up with interest, and listened to the music. Liam could sense trouble in the air, and in fact, Gerry achieved what he wanted; the girl's attention was directed on him.

'How long are you going to stay in Northern Ireland?' Gerry asked her eventually.

'Only for this term.

'Did you win a scholarship?

'No, my parents support me, but I need to find a job as well, alongside my studies. Do you know anything?'

'You could take up modeling at the Art College in Belfast. They pay quite well as I heard.'

'I wouldn't have a problem with that.'

'You're cool. My friend did for a while, too. He had to take loads of sedatives on the first day, when he started the job. He didn't want to get embarrassed in front of all the girl students for having an erection.' Gerry laughed. Judy was embarrassed. Lord puckered his eyebrows, trying to guess what Gerry was up to. Susan remained cool and looked at him very seriously:

'It's of no great importance. The body is only body.'

Gerry took the fife and played a few tunes, and then suddenly he laid it on the table. Susan took the fife into her hand with care and with amazement in her eyes.

'Who made this beautiful fife?'

Gerry replied without batting an eye:

'I did.' Susan laid the fife into his hand and looked deeply into his eyes.

'Very good.'

Lord looked at Gerry red with anger. Liam was bluffed himself; he could not say anything to this cheeky lie. Gerry just kept on grinning at Lord, Liam felt that he could have sunk into the floor he was so ashamed for his bro.

Unexpectedly, but with perfect timing, Susan announced that she had to make a phone call, but did not know where could she phone from. Gerry offered to show her to the next phone box in the street. They both stood up, Susan went ahead, while Gerry stepped back quickly to the table. He put down the fife in front of Lord.

'Nice piece of work, thanks.'

By this time Liam could see that Lord had given up on Gerry. He looked back at him pitifully, scaring Liam, but not Gerry. Liam realized that his brother had just lost another friend. He managed to get rid of Judy, too, who stood up angrily and hurried out of the place like a whirlwind.

Later, having spent two hours with waiting for Gerry, Liam went down and walked around in the park and at the shore of the river, hoping that he would find them. Finally, he found Gerry, sitting alone on a bench, daydreaming.

'What's wrong with you, Gerry?'

'I told her that I lied about the fife. She was pissed off, she had to go.'

'You're such a bullock. Lord's pissed off, too.'

'That was on purpose, I've had enough of him.'

'Have you had enough of all your friends?'

'I'm going away, Liam, and I won't need any mates there where I'm going.'

He took out a cigarette from his inner pocket and lit it. Liam felt completely powerless.

It was very scary that Gerry not only isolated himself from his friends, but also drunk and smoked drugs. On top of that he kept driving his motorbike. Their mother did not notice anything, neither Seamus; they only saw what they wanted to see. Liam felt that for their mother Gerry was the wonderful, talented older son, so much resembling of their father that she could only see their father's perfection in him.

Seamus, on the other hand, saw an indolent, spoilt youngster who did not want to communicate with him, who defied every approach, and he had given up on him years before, anyway.

There was only one occasion when Liam was so desperate that he had to ask Seamus' help. That night Liam had a dream in which he was in the desert. The sun was setting and parts of the sand hills were already veiled by darkness. Suddenly, a stallion rider appeared on the laced edge on the horizon and he recognized their father. A little boy was sitting with him in the saddle, proudly gazing into the distance. It was Gerry, but Liam could only feel this.

The next second he changed his viewpoint and he was sitting in the saddle, looking down to five women. They all wore long black gowns, but one by one, the wind uncovered their faces. Each of the faces had an aspect of CC. One had her smile, the other her blonde hair, the third had blue eyes, the forth her nose, they all reminded Liam of her and he felt love spreading all over him, opening his eyes to a different perception, mellowing his muscles and his joints.

Father handed him down into the hands of the first woman, who then gave him to the next one. One by one, they all kissed him and passed him on. Each kiss felt different, but deeply moving. He did not know whether to laugh or to cry. Then he looked up and he saw that Father was gone. The women started to giggle and kept giving him from hand to hand, and he began to feel dizzy from being passed on in this carrousel of love. He felt nausea and the world was spinning not only horizontally, but also upside down. He quickly and firmly told to himself that this had to be a dream and he could wake up, if he wanted.

He woke up. Gerry was shaking him violently. He did not

understand what happened. Gerry was happier than ever before.

'Liam! Bro! Did you see her, too?'

Liam could hardly form the words with his numb lips.

'Yes, Gerry, I saw her with your eyes.'

'She was beautiful, wasn't she? I'm so happy that you came to see her. She must have called you to herself, too. I have been there many times. This is how she calls.'

'It was great to see Dad.'

'Yes. He is there, too.'

'That's where you are going?'

Gerry did not reply just pushed a kiss on Liam's forehead and smiled. The little hairs stood up on Liam's arms and legs. He was shivering. Gerry, with his mind already somewhere else, jumped to his feet and left him alone, stupefied. Liam heard him taking the steps by two down the stairs to the lounge. He looked at the alarm clock. It showed five forty. It was very cold in the room and he longed back into the heat of the desert. Then he heard the ignition of the motorbike.

Liam's Choice

When Liam heard Gerry leaving on his motorbike he jumped out of his bed and ran down the stairs to the living room where Seamus was sleeping on the red couch. He often stayed overnight, but never slept with their mother in the same bed for reasons the boys could never grasp. Liam shook Seamus awake.

'Seamus.'

'What the heck? What is it, Liam?'

'It's Gerry. He's run away on his bike. Let's go, please, Seamus, let's go and find him.'

They sat in Seamus' car and drove in the direction where Liam heard the bike disappear. Seamus did not ask anything, he was still half-asleep. He simply accepted that Liam needed his help. Liam started to talk about the desert half to Seamus half to himself. He remembered the games they played there, when they were younger, how they used to scare Auntie Maeve with their hiding and disappearing in the back of the house. The battles and spying on the enemy, their common rescue searches for Dad, who was held hostage. Then he told Seamus about his dream that night. The reappearance of the desert in his dream was strange enough, but the fact that he really met Gerry, and became Gerry and saw why he was there scared Liam more than he could admit.

Seamus was murmuring some amazed remark how interesting it was if two people had the same dream at the same time, when they drove in the valley alongside the river Lurgan. The air became misty and suddenly, they could hear the motorbike approaching them from behind.

Gerry overtook them with immense speed. He looked back and laughed. Liam waved to him and shouted, 'Gerry, stop, don't go,' but of course he could not hear him.

Seamus accelerated and the car was dangerously speeding up, its engine roaring like an airplane, rushing into the mist that looked like cotton wool. Liam saw a rush of color, a patch of red on both sides of the road, and heard Seamus swearing and breaking ferociously. Then he heard the high-pitched horns of a train and he realized that the six o'clock express was approaching the railway crossing.

What happened next was like a film in slow motion. They managed to stop and the back of the car swung violently to the right. Gerry on the motorbike shot in front and Liam could see him looking at the train to his right with the same grin on his face that he used to put on when he was playing his silly pranks on his little brother.

Then the train arrived with a tremendous blow. They were lamed for about thirty seconds that seemed to be an eternity. They were waving in the wind and when the train finally left they looked anxiously over to the other side. The blood stopped to flow in Liam, and then it rushed into his head wanting to break out through the top of his scull like a geyser.

He saw Gerry lying in the middle of the road. The motorbike was hanging on a gorse bush, the back wheel still spinning. There was no collision; Gerry won the race, however the back blast that followed the train must have hit him from behind. The motorbike slid, Gerry flew out of the saddle, and the uncontrolled energy pushed the driverless vehicle up the side of the road.

Liam and Seamus ran over to Gerry. He was lying on his back, with arms and legs spread wide, his motionless face turned to the sky, his lifeless eyes open. The blow of the train cleared the air, the mist was gone and the sky was suddenly crystal clear. Gerry's eyes were reflecting the clouds drifting along in the pale blue of the sky.

This was not an accident, it was a conspiracy. The whole scene seemed like an ambush that was arranged to trap the brave knight rider: the mist, the train, the wind and the patch of oil precisely placed on the road. Having fulfilled their purpose the props started to dissolve. The train, its wind and the mist were gone; the dry mud that filled the ribs on the concrete soaked up the patch of oil. The wheel of the motorbike stopped moving. Gerry seemed to be smiling at the crescent moon that was still there low in the sky, waiting for her shift change with the sun.

Seamus checked Gerry's pulse on his neck and nodded to Liam to say that he was alive.

'He's unconscious. You stay here with him; I'll go and get the ambulance.'

Seamus dashed to find a phone box. Liam stayed there with Gerry, grabbing his hand, massaging it, and talking to him. He was not sure whether it was right what he was doing. He was acting instinctively. He could see that Gerry was on a journey in no-man's land between life and death, wavering, perhaps trying to get away forever. On the other hand, Liam was trying to keep him there with all his forces.

'Please don't go away, don't leave me. I need you, bro.'

In the back of his mind, behind the panic and the fear for his life he was amazingly calm and wise. He knew with absolute certainty that there is no chance, everything happens with a purpose. He knew that he would never want to go back into the desert, for that was not his world anymore. Perhaps, we all came from the desert, but we came here with a purpose. Liam knew with the deepest sincerity that he wanted to live life on earth, even if it hurt, for he had chosen to be born. He realized that his coming to earth had a reason; it did not happen as a blind hit of chance. His purpose in that moment in time was only and absolutely to save his brother's life and explain this to him with all his heart.

During this in the front yard of his mind he was anxiously repeating the words: 'Gerry, stay here, Gerry, stay here,' like a prayer.

The Last Ride

The traffic light shows green. Strange, that is my body lying on the road. My head rests in a puddle of oil on the concrete. Liam is holding my hand, but I cannot feel his touch, I only see what he is doing. Like a film. His voice echoes long after each word he speaks out. There is no pain. My eyes are wide open, but I see my face from far beyond. I look into my eyes; I could laugh now if this was not so serious. I stopped grinning; eventually I would not mind dropping the nasty habit once and for all. Liam is near to collapsing. He is repeating words that I do not understand. I would like to tell him that it is all well, for I am on my way to a place where nothing ends.

Crucial moments of my life appear in front of my eyes, hovering in a transparent cover like a soap bubble. Hurting words spoken out, thoughts and spoilt emotions. I feel them again, the pain and the bliss. One by one they disintegrate and become separated from each other, like colorful spots in a Persian carpet. You can only see the pattern if you distance yourself and go far beyond.

I hear or rather feel a voice. It is wise and caring and it tells me that Liam is all right. Then I see a stream of golden light and it loves me and I love it back, creating a connection. I let myself be taken away with immense speed to the land of gold where light pads me all around. It feels as if I had never known happiness before.

The golden yellow hills are in constant movement and I am riding my bike, spraying the sand under its wheels. I am able to hear the music that the running sand creates, the gentle melody of constant change.

This place is so familiar; it feels like my real home. I feel a deep connectedness to each and every grain of sand, the particles in the air and the photons in the light. I am limitless and happy. I feel an inner knowing; a promise fulfilled, and I glimpse CC holding our baby on her arms. She opens her mouth and I can hear the same soothing voice, full of wisdom.

'Gerry, you still have a choice. You can go back, if you want to.'

She gives me the baby and I look at this small bundle of light and I laugh. CC disappears, but there is still the voice saying:

'Life is much more important. That's where you learn forgiveness.'

I look at the bundle amazed, for I realize that it is the source of that voice. I open my mouth and say: 'Hello' with the same resounding, loving voice. I watch the wonder, as it elevates from my arms, opens its transparent wings, so powerful. It flies closer and presses a long and deep kiss on my lips. Then it laughs at me with the sound of a waterfall, and points at something with a tiny index finger. I follow the direction with my eyes and see CC again.

She is in Belfast, leaving a grey building, only the window-frames are painted blue. 'Brook Centre' is the writing above the door. She locks the door behind herself, and then pulls down a shutter. When she turns to go she notices the crowd waiting in the street.

They are carrying posters with images of aborted embryos. They shout and encircle CC, coming closer, shouting at her 'Murderer! Murderer!' CC is scared, and tears fill her eyes. I cannot let her cry. I give gas and the Triumph jumps off. The crowd shrieks back and opens in front of me, giving me way. I pull in on CC's side. She smiles at me and slips onto the seat behind me. We are riding the wind, her hair flies and I know that I am free to say 'yes' to life.

Leo's Initiation

Leo went back into the desert, as Saoirse advised him. He was expecting scorpions and snakes and death, for he had to fight with his deepest fears. He traveled around with the intention to ask him, what he wanted, but found no Devil. He saw his own shadow, however, the fear of being who he was. It took him a while to understand that he did not have to fight his instincts neither the love he felt for his beautiful friends. He knew that God had been trying to show him something, but unable to understand His message, he had been hovering around, exposed to destructive forces. God was omnipresent. Therefore, if there was a Devil; He was the Devil, too. He was just as much Leo's shadow as his light.

It seemed that he had been obsessed with his fears of the truth about his sexuality and being fixed on them he created the image of evil for himself. Yes, living life as a gay man would have been dangerous, but living was dangerous, no matter what. Admitting the truth was hurtful. He realized how deep was the division between the heterosexuals and the homosexuals, especially in the world he lived in. He had to stand to his truth; he realized that cheating called the calamities onto him, not the truth. He was much more than a gay boy. He was a talented musician, a creative being. He was very fortunate, for he had a means of expression, he could transform his struggles into art. He was the desert with its vastness and billion sand grains. He was a cell in God's body. He knew that he could return to the desert and he could get all his answers from there anytime, because that was the 'I' that he was.

From this time on he entered and exited these plains of consciousness with ease, and he was happier than ever. He felt stronger after each journey. He was well anchored in the desert, this place of constant change and steady movement. He did not meditate for longer than half an hour daily, but time had a different pace in the desert.

After a while, when he got rid of his fears about himself, he realized that actually those fears had kept him imprisoned in his lower self. If he was a gay man, if he ever found a lover in real life he would not become a 'cunt,' but a man who was physically drawn to the same sex. His spirit was free and beyond gender.

Dropping the chains of his fears he had the capacity to change form without losing himself and take on anybody's persona in the desert, if he so wanted. He could become CC with delight and Gerry with compassion and power. He slipped into the skin of the racing Gandhi once, just to find out that he could change forms as he wanted and he was not only Gandhi at all. He was Jesus, and Buddha and Mother Theresa and Joan of Arc, an endless series of lives and fates and expressions of life. The racing Gandhi was a messenger and in fact, he was Gerry's father just as well. He recognized the spirits of many great people, and he could be any of them.

It was amazing to discover that he could see down onto earth from the desert and with a distinctive sense he always knew whether something was happening in real life or just in people's imagination or thoughts.

He watched Gerry's accident from the plains beyond. He saw Gerry falling with the motorbike, the bike running from underneath him up onto a gorse bush and him falling on his back, hitting his head. Leo was watching from beyond, therefore he was not shocked, neither worried. Gerry left his body with ease and flew towards Leo. They smiled at each other and hugged. Leo felt immensely feminine and he was full of forgiveness towards Gerry. He confessed his love for him and kissed Gerry on the lips for an endless time.

This kiss was a revelation for Leo. It was so sweet and reassuring; he never wanted it to stop. He reached his tongue into Gerry, like the fangs of Medusa, searching, wanting to embrace, wanting to possess. Leo knew that Gerry was dying and he knew that he could keep Gerry there, in the desert, with him forever. Leo, being this feminine goddess felt that they could become each other's wonderful spouses and they could have created balance in their worlds for eternities. He felt so strong and sure of his truth that he thought he had all the power to transform it into reality. Leo became the primordial woman, the mother of all lives; who had the power to take as much as to give.

However, a male voice deep inside him warned of danger. If he kept him there he would stop the flow of all life in him as well, and all the other lives on this planet. He would freeze that moment and they both would become static, stony and heavy, for Leo would limit his own multidimensional perception to two or perhaps four dimensions, and eventually he would stop creating his own reality. Gandhi's beautiful Indian voice told Leo what he knew very well already: 'Real love is not grabbing, real love is letting go.'

Was it time for Gerry to die? This was the question. Leo could not find an answer, and he felt that he had no right to keep Gerry there, but neither had he the power to send Gerry back into his body. Gerry still had a choice of his own! Leo's experimenting mind wanted to find out immediately, whether all beings would have the same freedom at the moment they were about to die or only Gerry had this privilege. Perhaps this only happened with victims of so-called accidents, or God did not mind and did not care which side of his reality they resided in? Leo laughed, for he knew that he would evidently have to go his own way to find out and decided that he will watch and visit many men and women in this crucial moment of passing over, before he would try it out for himself.

Leo still laughed when their lips parted. Seemingly, he was a naughty fairy, in a way Gerry's child. He giggled and showed Gerry the way to CC, who was connected to Leo too, in a motherly way. She was wandering in the desert in her dreams. Gerry, riding his motorbike, entered CC's nightmare and saved her from the anti-abortionist protesters who were threatening to kill her with guilt and shame. Then Leo heard Liam's prayers who wanted to save his brother's life at the railway crossing in Lurgan. Leo kissed Gerry again and this time it was the kiss of life.

Epilogue

Gerry opened his eyes for a second and Liam knew that he had heard him. No matter how good it was in the desert he would come back. Liam felt relief that his brother loved them and decided to share his life with them. The ambulance arrived at the same time as Seamus. The paramedics gave Gerry an injection and took him to hospital.

Marie was terribly shocked; she fell ill with grief when the doctors told her that Gerry was in coma. It was more perplexing that the CT scan showed no evidence of a serious head injury to justify it.

Although he was certain, there was no way Liam could have explained it to a doctor or even to his mother that he knew that his brother was wandering in the desert, trying to find a meaning for all that had happened to him and Saoirse.

They had to wait for his return for a long time, though. Two years went by with everyday visits, readings at his bedside, talking to him, playing his favorite music. Liam got Leo involved and Lord; too, they even played their songs in the hospital. They tried all their means to wake him and bring him back, but they achieved nothing.

Their energy was running out and Liam could see Ma fading away with every visit, each day. He knew that he had to do something to save her and Gerry, too. She refused and was very upset by the idea of getting Saoirse to help them.

Since Gerry's accident his mother read all Saoirse's and Gerry's letters that they found in the house and she developed an awful hatred against Saoirse. For Marie she was the source of all evil, and her big son was the victim of love. Liam had to be very diplomatic. He had to fight for his truth to convince her, and he had to make her feel that she won at the end. Liam carefully avoided mentioning that Marie needed to be saved as well. She would have never admitted that.

Liam realized that it was better not to leave everything to chance, especially if it involved someone very important. He did not care whether his bro was going to be grateful to him after all, or he might never talk to him again, but he knew that they needed Saoirse's help to get him back. He wanted to save his brother, no matter what the consequences.

After a month spent with the agony of convincing his mother, she finally agreed and they asked Saoirse to come to the hospital. She was very embarrassed to see Marie again, who seemed to be blaming her with all her body language. Marie did not say a word, but the stubborn woman she was, she could not hide her feelings. Liam took Saoirse aside and told her that his mother would blame any girl; she did not mean it personally.

This was of course, a ridiculous lie, but Saoirse seemed to be more than familiar with human weakness, thus she understood. She showed so much compassion for the pain of their mother that Liam nearly cried.

Saoirse sat down on Gerry's bedside and started to talk to him. They saw no reaction on his face, but on the monitor they could see that his heartbeat was speeding up. Marie immediately warmed to Saoirse; she seemed to have instantly forgiven her. Liam and she were both very excited and stepped closer to the bed. Then Saoirse uttered a big sigh, bowed her head down and kissed Gerry on his mouth.

It was amazing. Gerry, like the sleeping beauty of fairy tales, opened his eyes.

The day Gerry returned from the desert seemed to fulfill so many wishes. For Liam, he felt that he grew up in an instant, but this was not at all frightening, on the contrary, it filled him with pride, not only for having saved his brother, but for having been true to himself. After all, that is the most important.